All It Takes Is One

All It Takes Is One

Hayden W. DeGrow

Self-published by: Hayden W. DeGrow

Dedicated to all those who need a voice

Contents

Dedication   **v**

1   It All Started With Spaghetti   **1**

2   Surf's Up, Belly-Flopper!   **8**

3   Living Life to the Fullest   **20**

4   A Different Kind of Drama Enters My Life   **31**

5   The Show Must Go On   **41**

6   The Intermission That Changed My Life   **48**

7   The Miller House   **64**

8   I Set My Sights on a New Life   **75**

9   They Came From Miles Around   **83**

10   I Begin My Fight   **92**

11   Because Brochures Didn't Feel Adequate   **109**

Contents

12 Cold Weather and Warm Company 119

13 So. Much. Food. 131

14 My Message Is Spread Further 143

15 Why Must History Repeat Itself? 152

16 The Capitol Gets Hill-Jacked 162

17 When Dad Taught Me That 'Words Hurt', I Don't Think He Meant Like This 171

18 I Step Up 180

19 A Leader's Work Is Never Done 188

20 A Speech Like No Other 199

21 Reflection: An Autobiography 206

The End

Family Trees 218

Colby's New Zealand Slang 221

Acknowledgements

About The Author 224

{ 1 }

It All Started With Spaghetti

The scene was just chaos. The football team was cheering heavily as they were pumped for their game versus Westview High. The nerds had taken over a whole table and were immersed in a game of Magic: The Gathering©. The cheerleaders were in line, gossiping over the hottest trends. In other words, it was a typical high school cafeteria at lunchtime. The problem was, for me, I had no idea where I belonged in the whole scene.

My name is Nicole Adrianna Grant, and it was my first day of senior year at Lincoln High School in the lovely city of San Diego, California. Why did I feel left out? Well, it kinda went like this. My dad was a navy officer and I had been in a lot of schools and countries throughout my life. My Kindergarten year was in Guam. I started middle school in Rio de Janeiro. I was a freshman at a school in Japan (and yes, I had to wear a special uniform; don't ask). But now, my dad was fed up with moving around and decided to settle down in a safe place, and San Diego was our place to live for good. My dad had taken a senior job that kept him in one place, and it suited the number of years he had given the navy.

Now, I know what you're thinking. *'Oh, wow! She's been everywhere! It was like living a twenty-four-seven vacation for her!'* But that is where you'd be wrong. Dead wrong. I was forced to stay on the navy bases all day every day, and it wasn't exactly a vacation. Monsoons, hurricanes, typhoons, earthquakes, all-day drills, and harsh characters made life hell for a kid. It also didn't help that there weren't very many other kids on the bases, and that left me very much alone for much of my adolescence. My mom died giving birth to me, so my dad had to raise me on his own. However, as he was in the navy, it was actually the various support staff on the bases that raised me. So, as a result, I was a bit of a tomboy and didn't have a lot of social skills.

Now, let's get back to that cafeteria scene. As I was walking through the room, I was not really sure of where to sit. I could almost *feel* the eyes of hundreds of kids staring at me as they judged me. I finally found an empty table off to one side, and I finally got down to the business of chowing down. The menu that day was spaghetti and meat sauce, so I was enjoying one of my favourite comfort foods when someone came up to me.

"Hey, mind if I sit here, dudette?" An accented voice asked. When I looked up, I saw a tall, lithe guy with a mop of blonde hair, blue eyes, and a tan that rivaled those of the locals I had seen in Hawaii. He was holding his own tray in one hand and his bag in another. After I indicated affirmative, he sat down across from me and continued. "You're a new girl, here, aren't you?"

"You got it, surfer." I said, shrugging. "Nobody invited me over to sit, so I just found my own place."

"Well, you do not have to sit alone anymore." Surfer-dude said. "You just made a new friend. The name's Colby, mate. Colby Anderson. What's yours?"

"Nicole." I said shortly, unsure what to say to him exactly. "Are you Australian?"

Rolling his eyes, Colby responded. "I wish people would stop assuming that. Dudette, I'm a proud Kiwi from New Zealand!"

"Sorry." I told him, throwing my hands up. "I was just curious."

"All good, girl, I get it all the time." He said, patting my shoulder. His openness was extremely foreign to me, as I was more familiar with strict, reserved men and women around the navy. "So, what brings you to our slice of California paradise?"

"My dad is an officer in the navy." I answered, wiping my face of sauce with a napkin. "He's now stationed here after being shuffled around the world like a deck of cards."

"Huh." Colby said, nodding. "We have a lot of navy kids here, you know. I could show you around and introduce you to them."

"No thanks." I responded, shaking my head. "I think I'll be fine."

"Okay, no problem, Nicky." Colby answered.

"It's Nicole, surf-bum." I snapped instantly, getting mad at anyone besides my dad who called me Nicky. "Nothing else."

"Oh, okay, sorry." Colby responded. Right then, a group of boys came by our table and began talking with Colby. I could tell they were a posse of surfer-dudes like Colby, due to their very casual language and body stance. As I polished off my lunch, I started getting ready to leave when Colby stood up too.

"Jackie, you and Pablo check the surf and see if we're a go after school." Colby was saying. "Frankie, you and Tommy go and talk to Laura and see if her pa will reserve our usual spot on the beach. I have something to take care of before lunch is over."

"You got it, *señor!*" The guy I assumed was Pablo said, saluting. As they walked off, I turned to Colby.

"What is that 'something' you needed to take care of, if you don't mind me asking?" I asked, frowning as I picked up my tray.

"You." Colby answered simply. "I'm personally inviting you to our senior surfing bonfire tonight as we celebrate the first day of our last year of being a kid."

"What?" I cried, utterly taken aback. "But I just got here!"

"Exactly!" Colby said. I could tell he was on the verge of laughter.

"How did you know I was a senior?"

"I saw you in first period, mate!" Colby responds as if it was obvious.

"But...why?"

"You need to feel like you belong, right? Well, this is your prime opportunity, dudette! We're always looking for new recruits and you're *perfect!*"

As I heard this, I looked down at my sandals and blushed. Shuffling my feet, I admitted quietly, "I don't know how to surf, though. I never learned how. I'll look stupid."

"No, you won't, because it doesn't matter!" Colby waved aside the comment. "We'll teach ya the way of the waves, mate!"

"But how can you be so nice to me when I was so mean to you just a few minutes ago?" I persisted, feeling very shocked now.

"Hey, trust me, bra, I've met far worse 'tudes than you. Just meet up with my peeps and you'll cool right off." Colby replied, putting his hand on my shoulder again. Normally, I would slap a person if they touched me like that. But Colby seemed to be harmless, so I let the gesture go.

As the bell rang, I finally said, "Okay, just let me confirm with my dad and I'll join you guys tonight!"

"Choice as! Meet us at Ocean Beach after school, and we'll give you a clique to settle into." Colby said excitedly, picking his bag up and patting me on my shoulder one last time. He then took off, heading to class.

As I tried to process what had just happened, I glanced down at my schedule and hurried off to my next class too. The next big surprise to me was the fact that I shared many of my classes with Colby or his pals. The rest of my day was spent in complete disbelief that I had already garnered the attention of a group, and they seemed to be popular with a lot more people than I initially thought.

In my fifth period physics class for instance, while we were copying down notes about what we were going to be learning in the semester, I saw him quietly chatting with a brown-haired guy named Julius. When the teacher took a break, I could overhear what they were talking about. Apparently, they were considering what food would be served at the bonfire, and couldn't decide on whether hot dogs, hamburgers or both should be served. As we were assigned an activity, I lost the conversation and moved on.

I also found out in my seventh period gym class that a lot of the girls were also heading down that night, including a pair of closely-aged sisters named Andrea and Aubrey. As I heard all of the conversation, I discovered that Colby and his pack of boys were treated as the hottest things in the school and were the subject of crushes amongst many of the girls. With that, and the fact that the surfer girls were also amongst the other cliques like the cheerleaders and the athletes, I began to realize that I was entering the coolest group of people in the school almost instantly.

This was a little problematic for me. See, because I never had very many friends on the bases, and the ones I did have I rarely got to keep them for very long, I had a hard time keeping friends. My dad and I moved around so much, my social skills were minimal, to say the least. As a result, I normally felt very awkward around people. Being in this part of San Diego, where everyone seemed to be welcoming, well, let's just say that I was completely out of my element.

As you might expect, then, the morning I had had that day was scary and I had been nervous about what I might encounter. It seemed I was becoming popular and I didn't even need to beg for it! It almost seemed too good to be true, and as I thought about the what-ifs, I realized that, if Colby had indeed been screwing with me, he probably would not have been so forth-coming of the possibilities. The school day soon came to a close, and I decided that this was well worth the risk if it meant I could finally have some friends my age for once.

After school, I called my dad at the base and asked him if I could join the surfers at the beach. He permitted me, as long as I wasn't out for too long. After assuring him I knew what a school night was, I raced home to drop off my stuff. After donning my favourite swimsuit, I made my way back down to the beach, where I saw a huge bunch of people gathered around a massive fire pit. Little did I realize that this night would be the start of something that would change my life forever, and in ways no one could ever have imagined.

$\{\,2\,\}$

Surf's Up, Belly-Flopper!

<u>19th February 2011; 1438 hours</u>

Coming home to the barrack my dad and I share in Singapore, I slam mine and my dad's front door. Tears streaming down my face, I storm up to my room, not wanting to speak to anyone. I have just come from the base's playground, and as there are no other girls my age on the base, I tried to have fun with the boys, but they teased me for doing so.

"Get out of here, Grant!" Bobby McCoy yelled at me back at the playground, shoving me off the play structure. "This is a boys-only group!"

"Hey, I can play here, too!" I shrieked back, trying to stand up but slipping on the wet grass and falling back to my butt.

"Bobby, Calvin, and I have claimed this playground in the name of those who belong here!" Devon Wilhelm shouted. "You don't fall into that category!"

"My daddy works here, too, you know!" I squeaked, standing up at last. My leg was sore, and I had a cut on my shin.

"Oh, going back to your wittle daddy, are you?" Calvin Hodgson

mocked, sneering at me. "You are such a whiny little idiot! Besides, your dad is a stupid weakling! I'm surprised that he's lasted this long!"

I launched myself at Calvin, wrestling him off the structure. After a few minutes of fighting, Bobby and Devon came in from behind me and pulled my pigtails back, yanking me painfully off of their friend.

"Get lost, girl!" Devon shouted, and he pushed me on my way. "This is a boys-only playground!"

I then raced home, sobbing the whole way. I passed by shops and markets, as well as many officers, but I didn't stop until I got home.

Back at my room, after a few hours of alone time, I stop crying, but I'm still feeling miserable. It was then that my dad comes back home, calling out to me, "Nicky! I'm home!"

I am feeling so bad, I barely register his presence. I just come out of my room and into our kitchen, where Dad and I have a simple dinner of Kraft Mac and Cheese and hot dogs. The whole time, I barely speak a word, and while Dad tries to spark a conversation with me, I don't feel much like talking.

After Dad cleans up the meal, I read a book in my room instead of trying to enjoy the beautiful Singapore evening. Soon though, I hear a knock at my door, and when I say come in, Dad enters.

"Nicky? What's wrong? You seem awfully quiet today."

"I don't want to talk about it." I answer blankly, not looking up from my book.

"I won't take that answer, my little girl." Dad says kindly, sitting down next to me. "What's really bugging you?"

Sighing, I put down my novel and reply, "I was bullied by the boys at the playground today. They called me a whiny little idiot and said that I don't belong on the base because I'm a girl."

"Well, I can tell you right now, they're completely wrong about that. Women and girls belong in the military as much as men do. Those boys were just being misogynistic."

"But they're the only kids on the Singapore base that are my age! Who will I have as a friend?"

After considering this for a minute, my dad wraps his arm around my shoulders and kisses my cheek. "Well, Nicky, remember, I'll always be here for you. If you want, I'll be your friend. You can be with me."

"I dunno, Daddy. I mean, the boys were also teasing me about 'going to my daddy'. If you and I get closer, it might mean more bullying by those misogo-whatever guys."

"Just forget those boys." Dad insists. "I'm getting a new job soon, so I'll be at home in the evenings. We can be friends then."

After thinking for a second, I smile. "Alright, Daddy. Let's be friends."

***

8th September 2020; 1612 hours

Walking across Ocean Beach, I counted about sixty people dancing and singing around the fire, which was about the size of a car. When I came into view, I heard Colby shout out to his friends.

"And here's our newest recruit, everyone!" He called, coming over and wrapping his arm around me. "Everyone, I'd like you to meet Lincoln High's newest senior, Nicole!"

As cheers went up, I was blushing right down to the base of my brown hair. As I was slowly introduced to the crowd, I tried to remember everyone, but it was just too much to remember at once. After all that, I was taken to a row of surfboards and told something I never thought I'd be given.

"Pick one, anyone." A girl, whose name I recall was Becky Miller, stated. Her luscious red hair was held back in a pony-tail, and her lithe figure made me feel like a steroid-user.

"But I don't want to wreck anyone's board." I said nervously, looking at Becky. When I saw genuine happiness in her brown eyes, I knew she wanted a friendship between us, but I was unsure if I could hold up my end of that bargain.

"Not to worry, these boards are communal from the local surf shop. Laura's dad runs the place, and he always lets us use the spare boards. Just find one you like, and he'll let you keep it!"

"Really?" I asked, once again feeling extremely surprised at the generosity in this community. "Alright, well, let's see."

After walking up and down the row a couple of times, a green board with an exotic floral pattern caught my eye. "I think this one is the best for me."

"Ah, the Tonga board. Nice choice." Becky said, smiling and nodding. "It's a rare breed. Plus, it's supposedly blessed with permanent good luck. Well, grab the board, because I'm teaching you how to surf. Let's hit the waves!"

"Great, let's go!" I cried, yanking the board out of the sand and charging towards the water. I was stopped by Becky, though, as she pulled me back.

"Hold on a sec, sister, we have a few things to go over

before we hit the surf. Come on over here. Let's learn the basics."

I then spent the next couple hours learning how to stand on my board, how to paddle out, and how not to make a fool of myself in front of everyone on the waves. As I went through Becky's routine, we both talked about our lives. To be true, though, she was doing most of the talking, while I was remaining quiet.

"Yeah, I'm the youngest of five kids, and the only girl in a crowd of men." She shrugged. "My mom is a very busy lawyer and it's hard to have mother-daughter talks on the phone. I feel like Lor McQuarrie from that old Disney show The Weekenders."

Though I totally could relate to what she was coming from, especially since The Weekenders was one of my favourite Disney+ shows, I still stayed pretty much in my own world.

"Hey, you alive?" Becky asked, nudging my arm.

"Yeah." I mumbled.

"Well, don't let me talk the whole time!"

"I'm just, well, scared." I admitted, not looking at Becky.

"I can understand that you're a little shy and uneasy because you've been suddenly thrust into this whole new world. I get that, we've all been there. But let me give a lesson in overcoming that problem."

"What's that?" I inquired, looking up to my new partner. I was still practicing how to paddle and stand up on my board, so I was prone on my board.

"Talk." Becky replied bluntly. "Just talk to us, and we'll describe how you do that if you're confused."

"Okay, first question. What should I talk about?"

"Well, start off by telling me about your past." Becky told me. "We'll see where we are from there."

So, at her behest, I told her all of my stories of being on base. After just a little exchange, I realized I had just made a new friend. The feeling was so new to me, I didn't know how to react. I just carried on with my telling of tales.

"What was your favourite place to live? After San Diego, of course." Becky asked me as she moved my arms to show me how to properly paddle.

After thinking about it for a second, I answered. "Singapore. Dad went there twice. Once when I was eight, then he went back when I was thirteen. The first time was not a hell of a lot of fun, with only a handful of kids on base and none of them liking girls all that much, but the second time allowed me to talk with more of the locals, and I learned a lot from them, including some social skills and how to do some various sports."

"Sounds cool." Becky said, releasing my wrists. "Now, let's see you hop up from prone to pose."

A little while after that, when Colby came by to see my progress, I couldn't help but get a little flustered. It must have shown in my face because Becky was glancing between us so quickly it was like she was watching a tennis match. When Colby went back to the surf, she started laughing.

"What?" I asked, smiling sheepishly.

"I couldn't help but notice something." Becky stated,

grinning a little. "What do you think of Colby? He seems to have noticed you."

"Um, well, uh, I don't know." I said, unsure of my feelings. "When Colby had introduced himself and had been so nice to me, I guess, well, I kinda...well..."

"What?" Becky pushed, giggling again. "Remember, you can tell me anything."

"Alright, I felt a spark there." I finally submitted. "I felt something that I had never felt before."

"It's called being in love, Nicole." Becky pointed out, putting her knuckles to her mouth to stop from laughing outright. "From what I've seen, you've felt a feeling of love towards Colby."

"Should I ask him out?"

"*Not yet!*" Becky said loudly, her attempts at stifling her laughter for naught. "Give it a bit of time for the feeling to become mutual."

"Okay." I said, giggling myself now. I felt my tomboyish attitude slowly beginning to trickle out as my more girly side came forward. "Let's get back to surfing, shall we?"

An hour-and-a-half later, Becky felt I was ready to surf. Problem was, it was already supper time, and I hadn't realized the fact that I was starving. As I sat down with Becky and Colby around the bonfire, we were served hot dogs, pop, and fire-roasted marshmallows. As I looked out over the ocean as the sun set, I was relaxed, happy, and finally feeling like I could lay down some roots here, yet another feeling that was unfamiliar to me.

After the meal was consumed and we waited for our

stomachs to settle, Colby stood up. "So, Nicole...uh, what's your last name?"

"Grant." I answered, blushing. Why hadn't I mentioned that before?

"So, Nicole Grant, I would like to formally welcome you to Lincoln High's surf club and swear you in officially as a Lincoln High Hornet!"

Amid more cheers, I buried my face in my lap to hide my blushing. My cheeks were so reddened that day, I was sure they'd never return to normal, and my blue eyes were so full of happy tears, I was getting thirsty again. The people on the bases had never given me this kind of attention (with the exception of my dad, of course), so I was thrilled to have people recognize me as cool, especially guys.

After a few seconds, I stood up and faced the crowd. "Well, I have to admit, I'm not good at speeches, nor am I used to this kind of attention. I was not expecting it so soon after arriving here, but I appreciate it. Thank-you guys for giving me a group to join and giving me a way to have some fun to have in my senior year. This is gonna be awesome!"

"Choice as, it is, dudette!" Colby said, stepping up and wrapping his arm around me again. He held up his can of cola and said, "To Nicole, and to our last year in public school!"

"Here, here!" The club cried out, raising their own cans in a toast.

We all then downed our pops with vigor and enjoyed each other's company. Becky, Colby and I sat back together and exchanged stories about ourselves and our backgrounds. It turned out that Becky was right: talking was helping me feel more relaxed in the group. In our discussion, Colby explained that while he was born in Auckland, his family moved to San Diego when he was a toddler due to a lucrative job his dad had with his tech company.

"What is that job?" I asked.

"Outfitting the old naval ships with new equipment." Becky answered, proving that she had known Colby for years.

"Hey, my dad is in the navy!" I told him. "I think I know the company! Kai Pai Tech, right?"

"That's right!" Colby replied.

As we turned back to each other's backstories, it turned out Becky and Colby had been friends since pre-school and had shared a love for surfing since they were kids. They both worked at a local fifties-style diner called the Vinyl House and were the co-presidents of the Lincoln High surf club.

"Yeah, I'm saving up my cash to try and go to UCSD for bio." Colby told me. "I'm hoping to one day be the dude that saves the coral reefs in and around New Zealand and Aussie by researching them."

"Well, I'm hoping to go to UCSF and join their earthquake research team. I love knowing about the Earth." Becky said.

"Cool." I said. "I'm not sure what I want to do after school. All I do know is that I am *never* joining the military like my dad. It's just too hard a life for me."

"I hear that, sister." Becky told me.

"So, what was it like growing up on the bases?" Colby

asked. "The way you've been saying, bra, it must not have been a fun time."

I tried, to the best of my abilities, to describe my time as a navy kid. While I made it sound like being in the navy was harsh, it really wasn't all *that* bad, but when compared to San Diego, it was hell.

After concluding my story, we all felt settled enough that people cleaned up their mess, gathered up their boards and stormed towards the water. My heart felt a ton lighter after I had gone through my life story, and now I realized that I did actually have some social skills. However, I felt I still needed to work on them, and I knew my new friends would assist me in that. With what Becky said were perfect waves coming in, I waded into the water, got onto my new board and suddenly got very excited.

"Time to see if I can do this." I muttered, my heart racing. As I got out to the surf, I stood up and promptly lost my balance, belly flopping into the wave. I surfaced amid a roar of laughter from my new friends, but I didn't feel at all embarrassed. I just felt the need to get back on my board and try again.

After a few more flops, including one time where I landed hard on my back, I finally managed to stay on the board the whole ride and got my first taste of surfer's thrill. After cheering myself hoarse on my success, we came up on the shore and gathered up close to the bonfire. As we partied some more, I got to know some more people, learned of some of the clubs I could join on top of the Surf Club, and got a true feel for the school.

As Colby and Becky began talking about their classes and comparing notes on opening classes, I leaned back and relaxed a bit, looking up at the stars that were dazzling the night sky above us. Right then and there, I felt that I finally could have a fun time in a place and have a little freedom, two things I had barely experienced on base.

Just as that thought came to mind though, I looked down at my watch and saw that it was nearly ten, and ten-thirty was my newly established curfew. Realizing that I was going to be late, I told my friends that I would see them at school the next day and took off for home.

After running for nearly half an hour, I got back just in time. My dad was home from the base and after catching my breath, I told him all about my first day.

"You are NOT going to believe this! I already have made friends, a club has already let me join, and I have learned how to surf, sort-of!" I said in quick succession, barely able to hold my excitement.

"Sounds like you've had a pretty busy day, Nicky!" Dad said, his smile broad across his face. While most navy officers never see this side of Rear Admiral Robert Grant, I was glad that he never brought his work attitude home with him. "So, which friends did you make?"

"Two in particular. A girl named Becky, who is an awesome surfer and a lot of fun! The other is a boy named Colby. He is a guy from New Zealand that loves nature and loves surfing!"

"Hmm, this Colby. Is he someone I should keep an eye on? Is he just a friend, or is he something more?" Dad added, his expression changing. It took me a second to realize what he was meaning, and I swatted his arm playfully.

"Dad!" I snapped, my cheeks reddening again. "I just met the guy!"

"Alright, just asking." Dad replied, raising his hands and chuckling. "Well, it's getting late, sweetie, you'd better get to bed. Goodnight!"

"Goodnight, Dad." I said, walking to my room. As I got ready for bed, Dad's words kept ringing in my head, and I couldn't help but smile a little as I thought them through.

Living Life to the Fullest

Life continued on like that for me for the next little while. I would go to school during the day, then join my friends on the beach for homework and surfing. I have no shame in admitting that my marks were never all that great while I was on base, as I tried but failed to show an interest in what they were teaching me. With the help of my friends, however, my GPA began to improve, suddenly making me feel a lot more interested in school.

My talents in surfing were improving too, as I soon discovered that it was very similar to skateboarding, a sport I had taken up when I was an eighth grader in Singapore. I also discovered that my talents as a boarder had a wide appeal with my new friends and I gained new respect from them.

As September crept on into October, the weather cooled slightly, but this didn't deter us one notch. Soon, I had earned a position at the surf shop, selling merchandise to tourists for Laura's dad. My skills at surfing were improving greatly, and with the weather being near perfect year-round, I saw no end to the season.

***

As we hung out more and more, Colby and I did begin to develop a stronger connection, but my heart was still nervous about whether I should ask him out on an official date. A bonus, though, was that he got a discount at the Vinyl House, and he used that fully as we went on various meals together. Initially we went with Becky, and with this I started to realize that I had a posse of my own to feel proud of.

Becky and I became an unstoppable powerhouse partnership as time went on. We sat together in class and at lunch, we partnered up for various school projects, and we went on girls' nights out on Fridays, where we hung out at not only the Vinyl House but also an old-style arcade. Our times at the surf were shrinking as school got more and more busy, but we still hit the waves as often as we could.

Colby, on the other hand, kept to his male counterparts for the most part, but we still hung out extremely frequently at the surf. He even proved himself as a friend one time after school when a pair of punks came up to me in the schoolyard and tried to fight me.

"So, Princess Wuss, I heard your dad is in the rankings of those water-whiners called the navy!" One of the guys, named Richie, was telling me. He had on an expensive outfit of artfully ripped and faded jeans as well as a Drake concert shirt beneath an open hoodie. He was clearly one of those kids that didn't care about how much money his parents made, just about making trouble.

Standing up from under the tree I was reading at, I looked Richie in the eye (or at least *tried* to, as he was at least a foot taller than me). "What's it to you, Captain Altitude? And what makes you think the navy is as sucky as you describe it, 'cuz it ain't!"

"Both of my parents say that anybody who enters the military are societal washouts that have no life. I guess you fall into that-"

He didn't get to finish his sentence as I leapt at him and tackled the jerk to the ground. As I pounded the big guy, however, his friend joined the scuffle, and soon I was pinned to the ground by Richie's pal. Richie stood up and wiped his bleeding nose and lip.

"A notable fight, but you're hopelessly outnumbered, weakling. I have some back-up, whereas you, on the other hand, have no one."

"Well, see, that's where'd you be wrong, mate." A familiar, accented voice said from behind me. As the punks turned towards the sound of the voice, I wriggled my way free and stood up, only to be greeted by Colby himself, his sleeves rolled up and his fists clenched.

"Get lost, Aussie!" Richie's partner yelled. "This ain't got nothing to do with you!"

"Um, how 'bout no, Derek." Colby stated bluntly, frowning in a way that showed he was hiding a lot of fury. "You right, Nicole?"

"Yeah, I'm fine." I said, standing back a little.

"Shut up, wuss!" Richie snapped at me before turning back to Colby. "Now, if you don't get out of here, Dumbass from Down-Under, you'll get the same as your girlfriend, here."

"Wanna hiding, punk?" Colby challenged, and suddenly tackled Richie to the ground, the second time he had suffered that move in a span of ten minutes. I then got back into the fight, bringing down the guy named Derek. Soon, we were on the winning end of the fight, with me having Derek in a leg-hold and Colby had Richie in a headlock.

"I've told you a million times, mate. I'm a Kiwi, not an Aussie." Colby growled, showing off a side I had never seen of him. "And I'm now telling you another thing, and I'd appreciate it if you reiterated this to all your stupid punk friends: no one, I repeat, *NO ONE*, hurts Nicole Grant on my watch. You do that, then you're just asking for trouble."

He then stood up and shoved Richie off to the side. "Now get out of here!"

As Richie and Derek took off, I rubbed my bruises and tried to feel better. "Thanks, Colby. I owe you a lot. You fight like a pro!"

"Chur, my friend, thanks." Colby said, giving me a friendly hug as I began to feel better. "My folks got me into wrestling from a young age, so when the season begins in December, I'll be wrestling for Lincoln as well as my usual surfing. I think the better question, though, is where did *you* learn to fight like that?"

"My dad taught me to defend myself after we were stationed in some pretty sketchy areas of the world." I explained, picking my books up. "Helped out a *lot* while we were in Rio. Can't trust a soul there when you're a girl."

"Interesting." He replied, as he put his handkerchief to my cheek, where I had some cuts. "Come on, let me take you to my crib. Let's get you cleaned up."

"Okay."

As we walked down various streets, I began to notice that Colby lived in a pretty, but nevertheless working-class, neighbourhood. With how Colby loved life, I began to appreciate his desire for a better situation than what he was in. When we came up to his house, which was a small bungalow, tan coloured with white trim, he directed me to the front door, which had a brass knocker on it. That knocker had the New Zealand flag on it.

"Ma! I'm home!" Colby cried out as we stepped inside through the door. "And that girl I've told you about has come to bowl round."

"No worries, Colly!" A female voice responded from a hallway that branched out from the hall we were in. "I'm just getting prepped for my slog!"

"Come on, Nicole, the loo is this way." Colby told me, guiding me to the bathroom. After he gave me some bandages and some skin wipes to clean off the blood, he led me to the living room. There, we occupied a pair of armchairs and we chatted.

"Yeah, I know it doesn't look like much, but it's home." Colby said, noticing where I was looking.

"It's far better than a lot of places *I've* lived in." I pointed out. As I looked over at a portrait of the Anderson family, I saw that Colby looked a lot like his dad, and his mom was a very pretty woman, but he had no siblings, just like me. "You have a lovely family and a lovely house."

"Chur, Nicole, that means a lot." He told me.

Suddenly, Colby's mom came into the room. She had a few gray streaks in her long black hair, but her brown eyes were full of warmth and love. She was wearing a black blouse and matching skirt. I immediately figured she worked as a waitress.

"Gidday, miss!" she said, her accent quite obvious. "You must be Colby's new mate Nicole."

"I am, Mrs. Anderson." I stood up and shook her hand.

"Please, call me Robyn." Robyn insisted. "Colby's said a lot about you."

Blushing, I looked over at my friend. He was smiling sheepishly, and not looking me in the eye. Grinning, I said, "I'll bet."

"Well, I've gotta get to work." Robyn said, hoisting her purse. "Your father will be home for dinner, Colly. It's za night so don't surf too long."

"I'll remember, ma." Colby said. "See you later."

"See you Colly. It was nice to meet you, Nicole!"

"Nice to meet you too!" I replied. After I heard the door shut, I asked, "Where does your mom work?"

"The Greystone Prime Steakhouse." He answered. "She's a hostess."

"Interesting." I said, nodding.

"Yeah, her university degree in accounting didn't fully carry over when we moved from Auckland, so she's been working odd jobs for years to save up enough money to pay for her schooling."

"I see." I answered, not sure how to respond. Looking closer at the photos, I only saw pictures of Colby. "I'm guessing you're an only-child?"

"Technically no, but in general, yes." Colby answered. "I was supposed to have a twin, but he didn't make it. So ever since I've surrounded myself with other guys like me to make up for it. Kind of sounds silly, right?"

"No, I think it's sweet." I told him, looking into his eyes. "I always wished for siblings myself, so I can totally see where you're coming from."

After a few more minutes of quiet talking, Colby and I took off. "Go get your togs on, and we'll surf for a few hours after supper, Nicole." Colby said, patting my back by the front door. "Don't let those jerks get to ya."

"Alright. I'll see you in a bit." I told him, and I took off for my house. I'll admit, I was so distracted by what I had gone through, I got lost quite a few times, and had to ask for directions more than once.

****

Life for me after that was going in a direction I had never expected. By the time Columbus Day rolled around, I was feeling very close to Colby, but I was still feeling skeptical about us dating. The two of us were hanging out together alone just as often as I hung out with Becky, and as a result my crush on him began to grow.

"Becks, do you think I should ask Colby out?" I inquired on our day off. The two of us were sitting on the beach, and I was staring out at the man himself in the surf as he performed some amazing stunts on his board.

"You know what, Nicole?" Becky told me through a mouthful of turkey sandwich. "I think this is up to you now. If you want to date him, and you feel that you know him enough to trust him, then you have my approval."

As Colby came onto shore, I was squirming around as I tried to decide what to say to him. As he sat down beside us, we started a conversation as usual, but my mind was so distracted, I wasn't very much into it. Inevitably, Colby recognized my uncomfortable persona.

"Hey, Nicole, you right?" He asked, picking up a can of cola.

"Um..." I said, unsure what to say. I then blurted, "Do you want to go on a date?"

Colby stared at me in surprise, while Becky had her face behind her fingers. I gave myself a massive mental facepalm as I regretted being so upfront (there's those stellar social skills hard at work!). After a few seconds, Colby responded with, "Straight up?"

"Um, well, yes. Yes, I want to know." I answered, my heart leaping to my throat and racing like a cheetah.

"Of course, mate!" Colby suddenly cried out, a smile spreading across his reddening face. "I've been wanting to ask you out for a while, but I've been unable to pluck up the courage."

My heart was relieved, and it sank back down to its regular place. "Alright, so when?"

Colby reached over and pecked me on the cheek. "How 'bout now?"

***

A few weeks later, mine and Colby's relationship had become common knowledge across the school. While the two of us tried to deal with this and build a good partnership, we still felt strong together. This was put to the test one day, however, when I was bullied by one of the cheerleaders, whose name I found out during the encounter was Parvati.

"So, I heard you're dating that foreign surf bum." She stated with her hands on her yoga pants-covered hips and a sneer on her face. She had a caramel-coloured complexion, black hair, black eyes, and, according to Becky, a black heart hiding beneath her green baby-tee. "Poor, poor, you. And here I thought you actually were showing potential."

Before I could shoot back with my own brand of sass, Becky retaliated for me. "Hey, Parvati, at least Nicole is dating a guy who can spell his own name."

"Ugh, yeah right! I'm amazed that surf-bum can even get to *school* every day without guideposts!"

"Well at least he participates in an *Olympic* sport, not one that, when a team wins, they are thought to be the "world champions" when we're the only country that plays it!" Becky retorted, her face really getting mad. "Now if you don't mind, my Mac n' Cheese is getting cold, and you're not making it taste any better."

Parvati had no response, except to grimace and walk away. Watching her leave, I gave a low whistle.

"What was *that* all about?" I asked, sounding very surprised.

"Ah, she's just jealous that you got the attention of the coolest guy in Lincoln while she's dating one of the big football jocks."

"Why would she be jealous?" I pressed, still confused as I glanced over at Parvati's boyfriend, Cornelius Bloos. He was a massive linebacker and had muscles that made the navy officers I knew look tiny. "And why did you say that particular insult? Aren't the football guys usually pretty smart?"

"*Not* Cornelius." Becky insisted, making a face. "He's as thick as wet sand. He's lucky to still be *on* the team. It's only his strength and, ahem, 'talents', that have kept him where he is. You've got Parvati beat a mile in the boyfriend department."

"Are you sure?" I asked, feeling a little more insecure all of a sudden.

"Trust me, Cornelius is dumber than the clams we bake at Ocean Beach, and she's not much better." She stated, watching with disgust as the 'proud couple' walked by us hand-in-hand. Parvati had her nose in the air as she went by, and I could tell she intentionally pulled him into that walk-by simply to show-off. "Colby, on the other hand, is smart, funny, *and* athletic. You've got nothing to worry about, girl!"

"If you say so." I sighed, glancing across the room to

Colby, who was talking with his buddy Tommy. "Colby is the guy I've always wanted to date, and the fact that he's got a plan for the future beyond the NCAA accounts for something, but that still doesn't mean that Parvati's words don't hurt a bit. I won't leave Colby or anything, but still..." I left the last part hanging, feeling angry at myself.

"Hey, do you honestly think that Adam and I got off to a perfect start?" Becky asked, referring to her own boyfriend. "I had doubts and misgivings too at first. But we still loved each other and today I can look back at those chicks like Parvati and Chloe and laugh at them as my relationship grows and they go through boy after boy. You'll get through it, don't worry."

"Thanks Becks, that really means a lot." I replied, feeling better.

{ 4 }

A Different Kind of Drama Enters My Life

As Lincoln High left Columbus Day behind, I decided to throw myself into another club and hang up my surfboard for a while. When the drama club opened up with a production of Footloose, I decided to sign on immediately. Colby told me he would never join up, but he supported my idea entirely.

"My sweet, I never knew you liked being a thespian!" He said after I told him. It was the day of my audition and I was super anxious. "You've been such a quiet girl since I met you, outside the surf club that is."

"Well, while I was living on base, one of the few things I did to pass the time was sing and listen to music in my barracks room. I also watched musicals and Disney movies all the time. One of my favourite musicals to sing along with was indeed the movie Footloose, so that is why I wanted to participate in our school's production."

"Well, all of us in the surf club wish you the best of luck!" Becky told me.

"Which reminds me, I need to run. My audition is in five minutes."

"See ya, babe! You'll be a star, I know it!" Colby said, kissing me as I stood up.

After racing to the theater, I arrived just in time. When my audition began, I decided to sing my own rendition of Bonnie Tyler's 'Holding Out for a Hero'. Despite me being a little winded due to my running across campus to get to the theater, I sang my heart out and hoped that I didn't screw up a single note. After the final chord, I looked at the casters and I could tell they were very impressed. As they talked amongst themselves, I couldn't help but feel excited and nervous at the same time. After a few minutes, the casters looked up.

"Well, Ms. Grant," said Mr. Katz, the lead drama teacher, "your talents clearly are exceptional. We have deliberated and it is clear you love to sing that song and most likely others. We would be honoured to have you play Ariel in the musical."

"Really?" I asked, surprised. "Just like that?"

"Well, we have had a string of auditions, but no one has shown talent like you."

"We have a system here at Lincoln, Ms. Grant." Mrs. La-verne, the singing consultant, added in. "We give call backs to those for whom we have a hard time deciding the role. For you, however, the decision is not at all in question. You have the part of Ariel no matter what."

"Really?" I asked again, my voice squealing as my excitement built up.

"Really." Mr. Katz confirmed, smiling. "Welcome to the cast, Ms. Grant!"

"YES!" I shouted, not believing that my first crack at being a performer was in a starring role. I charged out of the theater, jumping up and down in ecstasy. I had to run back quickly to grab my rehearsal schedule, and then I ran to class, my happiness so great, I might as well have had moons of excitement orbiting me.

***

The next few weeks were insane. Though Laura's dad gave me a break from my job so I could rehearse, I refused, saying I could handle it all. With that, I quickly became very busy. I still found time to surf, do homework, and work at the surf shop on top of all my rehearsals, and with such a tight schedule, I soon found that time was flying by. Before I knew it, Halloween was just around the corner, and not two weeks after that was when our opening night would be. Life at Lincoln High was perfect for me, and I couldn't imagine what would interrupt that perfection.

While rehearsing, I met a few more students outside the surf club, and they proved to be just as entertaining. One girl in particular, who was playing Ariel's best friend Rusty, proved to be very fun to work with. Her name was Samantha Isaac, and as we worked more and more together, we began to rehearse and memorize our lines together.

One particular rehearsal, we were reading our scripts and talking about our lives at the same time. It turned out that she also was very much into surfing, just not just as much as those in the surf club.

"Yeah, I thought of trying to get into that crowd, but their lifestyles aren't my cup of tea." She explained as we sat backstage. "I love the arts more, and that's why I'm more into the artist colony. I still love the sport, though."

"Well, hey, do you want to sit with me, Becky, and Colby whenever we have lunch off? We always have an extra seat!"

"We'll see." She said, just as the director called us onto the stage.

***

30th October 2015; 1818 hours

As I am sitting on our patio in Rio de Janeiro, I am waiting for my dad to come home so I can ask him a question. I'm watching a little video on YouTube, and I'm laughing all the way. I had just started at middle school, and I'm eager to try and get some friends at our new home. I am grilling up some beef and veggie kebabs for supper, and I am enjoying the smell wafting from the barbecue.

A few minutes later, as I pull off the food from the grill, Dad arrives. He was still in his fatigues, but the smile on his face was so warming, it made up for the colours.

"What smells so good over here? And where can I get some?" He jokes, sniffing the air.

"Beef and veggie kebabs Dad!" I tell him. "I used a new spice blend Lolly had created."

"Lolly? The little old woman down the street?"

"Yep! She and her son highly recommended it."

"Alright, let's try it." Dad states, sitting down.

We soon are trying out the food, which is super spicy but still darn good. As we work our way through the delicious meal, I decide to bring up my question.

"Dad, I know we have some traditions surrounding tomorrow night, but my classmates want to know if I'm available for a Halloween party. Taylor proposed the idea to me today at school."

"Hmm..." Dad is rubbing his bearded chin. He knows that, as I go to a public English-speaking middle school, I finally have some friends of my own. "Well, as Halloween is on a Saturday this year, we can still enjoy our standard traditions of the candy-corn eating contest and the prank-o-thon. When and where is the party?"

"It's at Jessica's house and it starts at 6."

"Well, as long as you are responsible, I can't see why you can't go."

"YES!" I shout. "Thanks, Dad!"

The next day, I am celebrating Halloween with my Dad as usual, and when I get dressed as Princess Mononoke (I loved Anime as a kid), I feel stoked for the party. After Dad escorts me to Jessica's house, I see a few kids walking around, but little as I am heading to Jessica's. As we get to Jessica's place, Dad leaves me alone, saying he would pick me up at ten. I walk up to Jessica's door, and Jessica answers almost immediately with a bowl of candy.

"Nicole!" She says, sounding surprised. "What are you doing here? And what are you wearing?"

"What do you mean? Taylor said you were holding a Halloween costume party tonight!"

"That's a lie! My brother's going trick-or-treating with my Mom, so I have to pass out candy!"

"Then what–" I begin, then I hear loud laughter behind me, and I see Taylor and her bunch of friends standing on the street with her iPhone displayed prominently.

"I told you she'd fall for it!" She screams. "You look so stupid! Nice outfit!"

As she and her friends run off, Taylor tries to say something, but I race home, completely overtaking my dad. When I get home, I burst into tears. Upon my dad getting home, he comforts me.

"I'm never going to another party again!" I sob, my eyes full of tears.

"Now, now, Nicky." Dad soothes, patting my shoulder. "Don't be hasty. We can just have our own party. And if you want to have one in the future, you can. You won't ever have to suffer this sadness again."

"Thanks, Dad." I say weakly, wiping my tears.

***

20<u>th</u> October 2020; 1210 hours

A week later, as Halloween got closer, I got excited for the holiday. Halloween had always been a fun time for me and my Dad, so I was stoked to see how it was done at Lincoln. I soon got my answer, as the school was putting on a Halloween Costume Ball on the thirty-first, but there was a problem: I still had no idea what to go as. Samantha, though, had apparently come up with a plan to amend that.

"Hey, maybe Mr. Katz will let us use the prom dresses

from the musical as our costumes. You know, promote the show and all that?" My new friend said as she, Becky and I sat down during one of our few free lunches together.

Snorting, Becky replied. "I doubt that. The school doesn't own those dresses, Sam. They're just borrowing them from a local theater company. Convincing him to let you borrow them for Halloween would be like trying to clean yourself by rolling in mud. Futile."

"That sounds like a bet." Sam declared, a grin sprawled across her face.

"You wanna make it a bet, Sam?" Becky asked, an equally evil look spreading across her face. "I will bet you a catered dinner courtesy of the Vinyl House for you and your cast if you can convince Mr. Katz to let you borrow those outfits. If you lose, you owe me dinner at the Vinyl House every day from Halloween until the musical is closed. Deal?"

Sam thought about that for a while. I could almost see the cogs whirring under her well-kept strawberry blonde hair as she contemplated the wager. "Deal. Get ready to lose a lot of money, Beckster, because you are about to see an expert in the puppy-dog pout in action!"

"Oh really?" Becky answered. "Suddenly, I'm just not that worried."

"We'll see." Sam replied, grinning further, and standing up. I stood with her, told Becky I'd see her later, and me and Sam made our way to the theater, where Mr. Katz was rehearsing with the boys. As they took five, Sam went up.

"Mr. Katz, can I ask you a mega-huge favour, please?" She asked, looking at him with massive eyes.

"What is that, Ms. Isaac?" Mr. Katz asked.

"Nicole and I are looking for a pairs costume for the Halloween Ball and we were thinking of using –"

"No." He responded tonelessly.

"But you didn't let me finish my request." Sam whined, turning up her pout.

Mr. Katz laughed humourlessly. "Do you really think that this is my first rodeo as a drama teacher?" He asked her. "I know you want to wear the prom dresses for your costumes. The chances of you returning the dresses undamaged are about as good as me directing a Tony-winning Broadway musical starting tomorrow."

"But...you can call me Trusty Rusty!" Sam countered, fully breaking out the puppy-dog look now. "Those dresses will not be damaged in any way. I swear."

"No matter how much you try to sway me, you can't guarantee me that those dresses will be returned in one piece. They are very expensive and irreplaceable. I'm sorry, but you're going to have to find a new pairs costume. No matter how 'trusty' you are, my Rusty."

Frowning, Sam walked away empty-handed. When she got back to me, we left the theater. As soon as the door closed, I said, "Looks like someone owes Becky a two-week dinner bet."

Sam looked over her shoulder and then whispered, "What, that? That was just an inevitable set-back. I am still getting us those dresses."

"How?" I inquired. "Katz is the only guy that has the key to the dressing room!"

"Not anymore!" Sam said slyly, holding up a set of keys on a ring. "Snagged these from the custodian!"

"Are you *insane*?" I asked her, never seeing this side of my friend. "Don't you think Katz will *notice* the dresses are gone?"

"Hey, it's only one night! He'll never know!"

"But...we can't just *take* them! They're not ours! We just use them because of the musical! Besides, Katz is one of the chaperones for the dance!"

"Actually, I heard word that he's not going to the dance. It's perfect!"

"No, it's not! It's stupid!" I argued. "You are out of your mind if you think Becky will let you win like this! Unless we get those dresses legitimately, I am *not* joining you in a paired costume. Becky and I will go. Good luck Rusty!" On that, I walked away, feeling bad for my friend but feeling good that I at least did the right thing.

As I continued on with my day, I kept glancing at Sam, but never said a thing to her. She didn't look like she hadn't done anything yet, but I wasn't putting it past her to actually steal her dress. As I was jotting notes in history, I was thinking hard about my costume. By the time the day was over, I decided it would be changed to a cowgirl. When I got home, I told my dad about the situation.

"You did the right thing, Nicky." He said as we ate soup and sandwiches on our balcony. "This Sam seems a little shifty to me. I'd stay away from her until this whole thing blows over."

"Planning on it, Dad." I confirmed. "I've had the school

life of my dreams up until now. Don't want some stupid mis-judgement on my part to ruin it."

{ 5 }

The Show Must Go On

When I got to school the next day for early rehearsal, I saw that Mr. Katz was in a *very* angry mood. After everyone had arrived, he gathered us together.

"Everyone, before we begin, I'd like to announce something. The dress that Rusty wears during the prom scene is missing and I would like to know what happened to it. Judging from what happened yesterday at the noontime rehearsal, I believe I know who has taken it."

Everyone looked around at each other, trying to figure out who the unknown thief was. I was on pins and needles, trying to decide if I should say anything. After a few seconds, Mr. Katz continued.

"I will give the person responsible one chance now to come forward and admit their guilt." He declared, looking at each of us. "If they don't, we will look through everyone's locker until we find the dress in question. Girls *and* boys!"

That last statement sent a chill around the room. A

minute later, Sam finally stood up. "Well, as you are pretty much aware of my request yesterday, I admit my guilt."

"*Our* guilt Mr. Katz." I said, making up my mind and standing forward as well. "I didn't actually do the stealing, but I encouraged Sam into making her bad decision. If you want to fire us from the musical, I will not blame you."

"Ms. Grant!" Mr. Katz cried, looking shocked. "Why?"

"We had a simple bet on whether you would give us the dresses or not, and when you refused, I taunted Sam into doing something rash. She stole keys from Mr. Clive and accessed the dressing room that way." I admitted, my head down and my heart sinking.

After contemplating this for a minute, Mr. Katz said, "Well, you two are very much guilty. However, I am happy you two were so upfront over what you two did. As a result, you will be punished accordingly. You two will still be holding your places, as it is too late to cast new girls for such important roles, however you will be receiving a month's worth of detentions each for this and you will not be attending the Halloween Ball. You will be here, cleaning up the theater for the musical with Mr. Clive and letting the stage crew have your tickets."

While everyone else blanched at the punishment, I succumbed to it. "Very well, we accept our punishment. Right, Sam?" I asked my friend, looking over at her.

"Yes." Sobbed Sam, nodding. "The dress is in the trunk of my car in parking spot eighty-seven. I put it in clear dry-cleaning bags to keep it safe."

"Very well, go get it, and return it to the dressing room.

I will notify yours and Ms. Grant's parents of this while you are gone. The rest of you, no more rehearsal for this morning. See you all at lunch."

As the rest of the cast walked out, I collapsed in sobs, feeling terrified about what my dad would say about this when I got home that evening. As I quietly cried, I heard a voice pipe up.

"Um, I know I am in no position to make requests here, Mr. Katz, but can we leave the police out of this?" Asked Sam, looking very much devastated.

After a brief pause, a line came from Mr. Katz that relaxed Sam a great deal. "Yes, we can, Ms. Isaac. As you are returning the dress undamaged and you fully admitted to stealing it, your punishment will only come from the school. Nevertheless, I hope you still understand the severity and the recklessness of your actions."

"I do." Gasped Sam, looking terrible. As she left to retrieve the dress, I left the theater, heading to my locker.

When I got there, I continued my sobbing, feeling like my new-found good life had just crashed down on top of me. Sam joined me a few minutes later and we just sat down on the floor and didn't say anything. We were just in our own little worlds of hurt, and we really didn't want to interrupt each other. I didn't know how long we were sitting in the hall, and I only looked up until someone tapped my shoulder.

"Hey, are you two okay?" Becky asked, a look of concern on her face. "You two look like you were both dumped at the same time!"

"We might as well have been." Gulped Sam, tears streaking

her mascara. "I'll admit to you, Becky, you were right. Katz didn't let me have the dresses, so I decided to do something a little...different."

"You stole them, didn't you?" She asked immediately, raising her eyebrows.

"Only one of them!" Sam said hastily, raising a finger. "But I did return it."

"So, does this mean you're out of the cast?"

"No, it's too close to opening day for that." I said, breathing heavily. "But we're *not* going to the dance, we're each getting detentions for a month, and we have to spend the Halloween Ball cleaning up the theater."

"Wait, what do you mean, *we*?" Becky asked, shaking her head. "Nicole, you did nothing wrong!"

"I told Katz I goaded Sam into stealing the dress, which is kind of an exaggerated truth." I explained, still trying to pull myself together. "I kind of helped Sam avoid jail time by showing Katz that she didn't act alone. I sacrificed my ticket to the dance for her."

As Becky looked carefully down at me, I had a feeling that our friendship was being tested right here, right now. After enough time to make it feel awkward, she glanced over at Sam then sat down with us. "That was a very noble thing to do, Nicole. You helped a friend you have only known for a month and lost your chance to dance with Colby at the Halloween Ball, his favourite dance. I officially call off the bet. Sam, you no longer owe me anything. I think you two are being punished enough for this."

"Thanks, Becks." Sam choked, looking better but still very

much in pain. "Well, I guess we'd better get to class. We still have school to deal with."

"True enough." I said, standing up to open my locker. As my friends left for their classes, I slowly tromped to my first period class, which was shop class. At least with that class, I didn't have to show my face too much to reflect my depressed expression of shame.

***

That night, I received a sound thrashing from my dad for not telling him the whole truth. He agreed with Mr. Katz in punishing me for my 'wrongful actions in egging on my friend'. I let him yell at me, as I felt I deserved it rightly. After about half-an hour, he finally stopped, and I actually felt a little bit better, knowing that the worst was over.

When I asked if I was going to be grounded, my dad looked straight into my eyes and said, "Fortunately for you, no. But you *will* be responsible for cleaning the house on your own this weekend and the next!"

Sighing, I nodded and went to my room. I sat alone and did homework, feeling bad, but also kind of happy that I at least helped a friend by doing this. As I finished my math work, I got a call on Facetime, and I found out it was Colby.

"Nicky!" He cried, sounding like he was in a state of shock. "Where were you this evening? You missed the best waves we've had in a while, mate!"

"Sorry, Sweetie, but I got into a lot of trouble today." I explained, not wanting to look much into the sad eyes of my boyfriend. I then launched into the story of what had happened, and why I decided to skip surfing.

"Aw, sorry, love!" Colby said. "Dudette, you did the right thing, saving Sam like that, even if it cost you. But I think it was worth the price."

"Thanks, baby, that makes me feel a little better." I told him. "Now, if you'll excuse me, I have a science project to plan, so I'll see you tomorrow, alright?"

"You got it, babe." Colby told me, blowing a kiss my way, then signing off. As I put down my phone, I couldn't help but smile for the first time that day.

***

The next three weeks went by without a mention of the incident. Even mine and Sam's cleaning on the night of the Halloween Ball didn't even jostle us to bring it up. The rehearsal schedule made school hard for me, and I never even saw the beach for the longest time. School was getting crazier with larger projects and heavier essays, plus my job was getting tougher as the winter tourist season was coming soon. All in all, I had little time to think, let alone feel good about my decision.

The night before the opening night, however, I was finally given a reprieve and I made the most of it by hitting the beach with my friends. With the waves perfect and our grub cooking on all cylinders, I could finally relax. While I rested on the beach, Colby came up to me and asked an unexpected question.

"Hey, babe," He said, holding out his hand. "I believe we missed out on something at the Ball. Care to dance?"

Looking into his eyes, my heart melted. "I thought you'd never ask."

As we slowly circled on the sand, dancing to the music playing in our heads, our friends were smiling and watching us. The whole time, I couldn't think of a better place to be in than leaning against Colby's shoulder in the sunset colours of SoCal. What I didn't realize was that this would be the last night I would smile or feel relaxed for a very long time.

$\{\,6\,\}$

The Intermission That Changed My Life

<u>19th, November 2020</u>

Opening night had arrived. As my fellow cast members and I got ready for the night, I was feeling extremely excited for what was coming up. I was so much so that I had a hard time concentrating on class that day, even if it was a Thursday. I got so dazed that when I was in physics class, my teacher had to call my name apparently *six* times before he could get my attention on the nuclear fusion concept we were discussing.

"Nicole!" Mr. Brock yelled on that sixth time. "Are you here on Earth or on *Venus*? I asked you a question and I would like you to answer it!"

"I'm sorry sir, I just am so excited for the show tonight that I can hardly focus today." I apologized, shaking my head to clear my mind. "What was the question?"

It carried on like that all day, with the exception of gym

class, where the volleyball we were playing that day kept my mind on task. As the classes ended, I raced to the theater to change into my first outfit and get my makeup done. My fellow actresses were equally as excited, but the upcoming show wasn't the only thing that was making me excited. I had gotten a surprise at lunch, with Colby and Becky telling me that they had bought tickets for my opening night so they could watch me perform with my dad. Though I was initially embarrassed, I soon felt like they truly wanted to watch me.

As the musical began, my heart couldn't stop fluttering. I have no shame in saying that I rarely got in front of people and publicly spoke or performed, so this was going to be another new experience for me.

As I watched our Ren, played by a guy named Jeff Coborn, talk to his Chicago friends, I whispered to Sam, "We are *so* lucky that Mr. Katz let us stay."

"No kidding." Sam breathed; her eyes focused fully on Jeff. I had noticed that the two of them were developing a relationship by working together. Though Jeff and I were technically the 'love birds' of the show, the kisses we shared were faked and I encouraged Sam to try and get Jeff to like her more.

As my first scene began, I was feeling so nervous, I nearly forgot my lines, but I calmed down and threw myself into the role. My songs were performed greatly, and I finally got to show my friends and my Dad, who also was in the audience, of what I was capable of. My song 'Holding out for a

Hero' was my favourite part of the act, as singing my heart out sent my initial stage-fright flying out the window.

As the first act went by without a hitch, intermission was called, and I began to relax even further. Suddenly, as I fixed my mascara in the dressing room, I heard a commotion happening out in the auditorium. Then I heard a blood-chilling sound: a gunshot.

***

<u>14th, August 2017; 1345 hours</u>

Dad and I are sitting on a beach towel on the shores of the Persian Gulf, enjoying some sandwiches and iced tea when an idea comes to mind. It is a beautiful day, with clear skies and lovely waves. There are some people enjoying surfing, while others, like us, are just sitting on the sand and chilling. Though I know it would spoil the day, I decide to ask Dad a question which has been on my mind for months.

"Dad, I love being here in Bahrain, but are we ever going to be in the United States?" I inquire, my smile falling slightly. "I would love to be in America, where there are more naval stations and bases to choose from and I can actually talk to the locals. Can you arrange that?"

"Nicky, I would love to say that I could, but it's not entirely up to me." Dad responds, his smile fading too. "But it may be possible soon."

Suddenly, a rarely heard alarm begins blaring. Dad quickly shoots to his feet and looks back towards the base, where the attack siren is ringing.

"Nicky, get back to the barracks!" He orders. "Don't deviate from our usual path, and don't attract attention to yourself!"

"You got it Dad!" I say, shooting to my feet and running up the beach.

Hauling ass to get back, I am racing hard to return to our barracks. When I turn a corner, however, a pair of black-clad terrorists are blocking the road. They're shooting large rifles everywhere, and I quickly turn around to head to a shortcut I know. However, they spot me and begin shooting at me.

Ducking behind a garbage bin, I hear bullets flying by me. I am truly terrified and am unsure about what to do. All of a sudden, just as quickly as I found myself in the horrible situation, some help arrives in the form of soldiers. As they take down the terrorists, I'm breathing heavily and whimpering, my arms covering my head. As the soldiers come over and take me home, I can't help but feel continuously terrified.

"Nicky!" Dad cries, looking relieved as I come in through the door of our barracks. "Are you okay?"

"She's fine, Captain." One of the soldiers says, patting my shoulders. "Just shaken up."

"Alright guys, you're dismissed."

As the soldiers salute and leave, I am sobbing and promptly jump into my Dad's arms. "Dad, I'm scared. I was so scared. I'm sorry."

"I'm the one who should be apologizing, Nicky. You're right. We need to find a safer place to live. And I think I have just the right place."

***

When a second and third gunshot were heard I shot up and took off, racing towards the door. As the other girls and the female teacher in charge of us dove under the makeup tables, I slammed open the door. Though I heard the teacher behind me desperately calling me back, I ignored her and burst out of the room. Charging onto the stage, I arrived in time to see a twenty-something-year-old man with a rifle shooting at the audience. My fear of guns and gunman started to come back, but as he turned his gun into the section Colby, Becky, and my Dad were seated in, I stormed in his direction. As I ran, he took aim.

"No!" I screamed, knowing what could happen. Despite my outburst, he didn't hear me, and began shooting. I could tell his shots hit their mark as the crowd screamed and dispersed, running for the exits. I looked up to the doors, but I saw that they were closed, and judging from the cues in front of them, they were also locked.

I charged towards the gunman, and when he spotted me, he turned onto me and fired, hitting me in the shoulder. Pain exploded all along my right arm, but I didn't let it stop me. I jumped off the stage and tackled the man, trying to prise the rifle from his grip. He quickly got me off of him, using a punch to my new wound as a means to weaken me. He then stood up, reloaded his gun, and continued firing upon my classmates.

"Oh no you don't!" I snarled, scrambling forward from my chest and taking out the gunman's feet. This time, he dropped his gun and I quickly got on top of it. As I stood up,

I could barely hold the gun due to my shoulder, but I aimed it as best as I could at the gunman.

"Shut up and hold still." I growled, my face tightened in fury. I then called out to the crowd, "Someone call 9-1-1! Get an ambulance here, quickly! And let's get GI Jerk-Face into a safe room."

"You've got no idea what I've got, bitch." The gunman snapped, speaking out for the first time. With that he jumped up and pulled out two grenades. He yanked out the pins and threw the baseballs into the crowd. One landed in the aisle behind me and the other landed behind the front-row.

"You ass!" I shouted, and dove down to the ground, leaping into an opening that went under the stage. I hardly had time to close the thin cover before the grenades exploded with a pair of loud bangs. The blasts sent shrapnel across the auditorium, and I felt small particles pepper my back, which burnt like I had just fallen on hot coals. At the same time, the stage above me cracked open like an old crate.

When I realized nothing was happening, I climbed out, grunting from my immense pain. As I stood up, I saw that the gunman was dead. He had been hit directly by the aisle grenade's shrapnel and was lying in a pool of blood. The stage was in ruins, as well as most of the front row of seats.

Most of the people who had escaped the gunshots and grenades were on the ground, or in shock. As I looked around, I saw that several of my fellow cast members were finally coming out of the dressing rooms. As I saw their mouths move, I realized I couldn't hear anything. But that didn't matter much, as I suddenly collapsed right then and there. After a few seconds, I blacked out.

***

I awoke in a quiet but busy hospital room, with Sam and a nurse beside me. I had an IV in my arm, and I could feel bandages all over my back. My shoulder felt better, but it still felt like a two-ton parrot was sitting on it. I soon discovered that I could hear again, but barely. As I tried to move, the nurse stopped me.

"Miss, try not to move." She said, her calm voice barely audible to my ears. "Your shoulder is going to need some healing time before you can move it."

"What happened?" I croaked, my memory a little fuzzy and my throat feeling terribly dry.

"Let's not talk about that right now." Sam said, her voice trembling, as if the memories for her were scary enough. "The only important thing right now for you to know is the fact that you're alive."

"Alright, can you at least tell me why I'm in a hospital bed?"

"Well, you have suffered over sixty serious lacerations to your back, which we have since cleaned up. Plus, your ear drums were ripped so your hearing will be reduced for a bit." The nurse explained, checking my vitals and entering them onto my sheets.

"What about my shoulder?" I breathed, my lungs feeling

like they were made of paper. My arm was in a sling and when I shrugged a little, I felt stitches, plus a twinge of pain.

"No bones were hit, but you got some tissue damage." Sam told me. She wanted to be a nurse herself next year, so she had become a walking encyclopaedia of medicine.

"Okay, thanks." I said. My neck cricked when I tried to look at Sam properly, so I tried to sit up. When I did, my shoulder flared with extreme pain. I had had broken bones before, but this pain was on a completely different scale.

As I gasped out in pain, the nurse softly yet firmly pushed me back down and said, "I told you to take it easy, miss. You're lucky you can still use your arm. Here, let me raise your bed."

As I tried to imagine a life without being able to use my arm, the nurse used a remote on my bedside table to raise me into a sitting position. When I finally could look around, I glanced over at Sam. It was then that I saw her still wearing the outfit she had on at the end of act one, but it was now wrinkled and dirty. She had circles under her eyes and looked like she hadn't slept soundly since the incident. It was clear she hadn't left my side the whole time I had been in the hospital.

"Have you gone home at all since I got here?" I inquired, calming down further.

"Not really." Sam admitted, squirming. "I have been snoozing sporadically while waiting for you to wake up. My parents understand, and I haven't even put on the change of clothes they brought me."

"I feel like I should be honoured, but I am a little grossed out at the same time." I responded, giggling.

Laughing, Sam said, "Yeah, I guess I can change now."

She stood up and headed to the bathroom. While the nurse filled out her final checks and moved on to the other patients, I followed her to the other people in my room. I was sharing it with four other occupied beds, everyone else in a similar situation as I was. I saw a couple broken limbs, and someone in a neck brace. I slumped into my bed, feeling relieved that I was at least alive. Looking beside my bed at the table on my left, I saw a stack of cards, piles of flowers, and a veritable circus worth of balloons saying get-well.

When Sam returned, wearing a plain white blouse and a denim skirt, I nodded towards my nightstand. "How long have I been out?" I asked, feeling like it had only been a couple hours.

"Today is Saturday, so it's been two days." The nurse said, returning to me. As I finally got a good look at her, I saw her nametag declared her as Terri. She had curly black hair, dark skin, and brown eyes full of sympathy. "You've been in and out of surgery to help fix your shoulder and to remove the shrapnel in your back. Your ears should feel better later today."

"Two *days*!" I cried out, my throat and ears screaming in protest again. "It only feels like a couple of hours!"

"Anaesthesia and unconsciousness do that sometimes." Sam said, shrugging. "You just got out of surgery about two hours ago. I had a feeling you would finally wake up fully tonight."

"*Tonight?*" I asked, this time more curious than shocked. "What time is it? Come on, help me reset my internal clock!"

"It's about quarter after ten in the evening." Sam told me, showing me her watch.

"Okay, next question." I continued, calming down and taking a swig from the decanter of water beside my bed. "Where am I exactly?"

"Kindred Hospital." Terri explained, checking on my IV machine again. "Surgery recovery ward, where you'll remain until you've been discharged."

After writing something on her clipboard, she looked up to my face and finished with, "I have others to get to tonight, but I'll be back in a bit. See you soon, Nicole."

"Okay, see you." I said.

*****

That night, I had a vivid dream. I was in the audience at the musical, and the gunner was in the middle of his shooting. As I glanced to my right, I saw Colby, Becky and Dad standing up to escape when the gunman took aim towards us. I then saw myself on the stage, yelling "No!", then shots rang out in our section. Dad dove on top of my friends, shielding them from a barrage. Shots hit him and I screamed.

"Dad!" I cried out, waking up suddenly and sitting up so fast, I almost ignored the pain exploding from my back and shoulder. My dry throat burned in protest to the stress.

Terri came racing in, worried about what had happened. "Miss Grant, what's wrong?"

Breathing heavily, I told her. "I dreamt about the gunman shooting into the section my dad and my friends were sitting in. I have to know, did they survive?"

"Nicole, I don't think I can say anything about that. You'll have to wait until your grief councellor comes in the morning to discuss that."

"Alright." I nodded. I lowered myself back to prone and I went back to sleep.

***

A couple days later, I had gone through a little bit of grief counselling, and the police had talked to me about the incident, but I still had not heard exactly who had survived or not. Sam had been coming back every evening, sometimes with a couple of my surfer friends. Tonight was no exception. As they made my time more comfortable, I began to feel a bit better about what I had seen. Around nine, the others went home, but Sam stuck around and the two of us began to talk about the shooting, as the grief counsellor had said that talking about it with someone was good for me.

"Nicole Grant, I'll say it again, that was either the single bravest thing I have ever seen someone do, or the craziest. You have made your dad proud!" Sam exclaimed, nodding proudly.

"Thanks, that feels good." I said, my face glum. "Sam, I have to know. I saw the gunman shoot into the section my dad was sitting in. He was with Colby and Becky. I'm having nightmares about the incident, and they're keeping me up. I think knowing the outcome will stop them. Did they survive?"

"I don't think you should-"

"I think I can handle it." I insisted. "I'm tired of being in the dark of my dad's and friends' conditions. Now, are they alive or not?"

Sighing, Sam looked down. As I frowned at her, I said, "Sam! Did they survive?"

As she looked up, Sam's expression was enough of an answer. "I'm sorry, Nicole, but none of them did. They, along with thirty-five others, are dead. You included, there were seventy people injured, many of them severely. The police are investigating the incident as we speak."

I didn't listen to the last two sentences. My heart sank so far, I wailed out and broke down into tears, crying hard. I thought I'd be able to take the shock, but I was completely wrong; my heart was shattered. Sam carefully and kindly hugged me as I sobbed, comforting me in my grief. I had just gone from being on top of my world, with a boyfriend, many friends, a father that was finally acting as such, to losing everything. I was an orphan, with almost no one left to love. My father was the only person I had ever gotten to know personally before Lincoln High, and the only loved one I had ever had before Colby, and now they both were dead. I felt hollow and empty, and it seemed like nothing in the world mattered.

"Listen, Nicole." Sam said gingerly. "I went looking for them after the shooting. Your dad died trying to protect our friends. He was shielding Colby and Becky from the shots, like a blanket. He died a hero. Unfortunately, the bullets also hit Becky and Colby. The Navy is praising him and you for your guys' heroics. Apparently, the admirals are even giving him the Purple Heart!"

"I don't care." I snapped. "Tell them to keep it."

"Come on, Nicole, you yourself are also getting massive praise from the police for your bravery." Sam countered soothingly. "They recognize that the gunman may have killed everyone in that whole theater if you hadn't stopped him! You didn't even let a shot to your shoulder stop you!"

"I guess." I said. I still felt horrible, but I had pulled myself together enough to think clearly. I realized that Dad would not want me to cry but to keep myself together for my friends. Though the grief was still hurting me, the part of me that had embraced the militaristic part of my childhood came out. I decided to recognize, but not fall victim to, my saddened emotions.

"What of the gunman? Do we know why he did this?" I asked, changing the subject and hoping for some answers.

"Not yet." Sam replied, shaking her head. "They at least identified him yesterday, though. His name apparently was Carl Fillmore."

"Can't say that that name rings any bells." I admitted, shaking my head. "Are there any leads on a motive? Or where he had gotten the weapons?"

"He apparently got the gun from a Cabela's in Oregon and made the hand grenades himself from old movie props and gunpowder."

"Gunpowder?" I asked, surprised. "Wait, if all those people

died, including the shooter, why didn't I? Not that I'm complaining, but you'd think the shrapnel would have pierced the wood and hit me harder."

"Keep in mind the surgery you had to go through." Sam pointed out. "You still did suffer severe hits to your back. Plus, you did hide behind the stage front, which is thick, solid plywood. You made it, but just barely."

"Thanks." I replied. "Going back to the shooter. What is known in terms of a motive?"

"His motive is still unknown, but he went to Lincoln years ago so that's something." Sam answered, shrugging half-heartedly.

"I suppose." I said, sighing. Despite my best efforts, my emotions suddenly returned, and I began sobbing again. "Sam, what am I going to do? I'm only seventeen. My eighteenth birthday isn't until February! I'm now an orphan! I have no immediate relatives that can be designated as next-of-kin! I'm on my own!"

"No, you're not." A new voice declared firmly. I looked over to where the new voice had come from, and I saw a woman standing at the door. She looked very much like Becky, but had a more lined face, green eyes instead of brown, and had gray streaks in her red hair. She was dressed in a pin-striped suit and was carrying a briefcase.

"Are you Becky's mom?" I asked, never having met the woman in person.

"Former mom, remember." She said solemnly. "Theresa Miller's the name. Rebecca Miller, or Becky as you knew her, was my only daughter. You, Nicole Grant, have also just lost your own dearly loved one. Over the past few days, I have been discussing with my fellow lawyers, and it looks like there's a good chance that I can do something that I have wanted to do since the shooting. Now, I can finally tell you what I've decided on."

"And what's that?" I asked, frowning.

"I want to adopt you as my new daughter. Our house is feeling a little empty without Becky, and you seem to be a perfect match."

I was shocked. My mouth hung open in complete surprise over what I had just heard. "But...why would you do this? You've never met me before!"

"Be that as it may, Rebecca had still told me a lot about you over the past few months. You sound like you are just like my late daughter and would not be against living with a houseful of men. Besides, I may be a busy woman, but that doesn't mean that I can't feel compassion towards someone that is in need, especially when that someone saved lives. You are indeed a spirit similar to my Becky, so I think you'll fit in perfectly in my home."

With that, my shock turned into genuine love. As I looked into the woman's eyes, I saw that she was probably as shattered as I was; she was desperate for me to say yes. "You are truly going to do this for me, Mrs. Miller?"

"Call me Theresa." She told me simply. "And does this answer your question?"

She handed me a piece of paper, and when I read it, it was a custody form. As I read it carefully, I realized that

Theresa wasn't kidding. The form was one from the government, transferring me to her family.

"I don't know what to say. I don't even think 'thank-you' would cover this!" I told her, my eyes tearing up.

Sam, who had remained quiet during this whole exchange, spoke up. "I don't think you even *need* to say anything, Nicole. Theresa, are you completely serious about this?"

"Absolutely." She responded, turning from me to Sam and back. She then smiled fully, and my friend's visage seemed to appear in front of me. "Welcome to the Miller clan, Nicole!"

{ 7 }

The Miller House

The last couple days of my hospital stay were far more hopeful and happier than my first two ever were, but there were still some obstacles. I was frequently visited by people, particularly my new brothers. Marcus, Samuel, Anthony, and Allan all came and met me the day after Theresa had come by, and, for the most part, it was a great little party.

Allan, the youngest, was nineteen and a college freshman studying mathematics. Samuel and Marcus, who were the oldest and twins, were thirty and were already out on their own. They both were science graduates, Marcus in chemistry and Samuel in biology. The two of them had a few young kids between them and, after hearing about them, I was *so* eager to meet the little rascals. Anthony, on the other hand, was twenty-three and very close to graduating from college. He told me he was a history major, which very much interested me, as I loved learning about the past.

All of the brothers had red hair like Becky and were bestowed with either brown eyes or green eyes, or, in Allan's case, both green *and* brown. Their personalities all varied in detail, but generally fell under the same category: athletic but gentle. It may be a rare combination, but I was grateful I would finally have people my age to compete with, but that would at least be fair at the same time. A bonus was that all of them were surfers and were eager to see me on the waves.

From what I heard from my new siblings, Becky was considered the baby of the family and the most beloved of all of them. This is what caused me some rifts. Marcus, Samuel, and Anthony were happy to have someone to fill a void in their hearts, but Allan took some convincing. When he had first visited me, he hadn't said a word to me, even when I tried to address him directly.

The second visit was with his mother and Marcus, so he was prompted to speak a little bit more. When we started discussing his studies, he began to warm up to me, and he explained why he was so resentful before.

"Becky was my closest friend, mainly because we were the closest in age." He described, wringing his hands. "No matter what happened at school, she was there for me. I never had many friends when I was a kid, so Becky was the closest thing I had. No offense to you, but no matter how deeply you integrate yourself, you'll never really be Becky.

My heart made me feel like I was invading the family. My head sinking, I responded. "I understand, Allan. I'm not trying to replace your sister, at least not fully, but maybe spiritually. I know that there will never be another Rebecca Miller, but I know that I'll do my best to try and heal the pain in your heart."

"And I think you'll do just that, in time." Theresa injected, her tone showing that she wasn't too happy with her son's feelings about having me as a new sister. "Allan, we both have work tomorrow, so why don't we leave your sister with Marcus and we'll get going."

"Alright, Mom." Allan said, standing up. "See you guys."

"See you at home soon." Marcus said. "The doctors said yesterday that Nicole, here, could be discharged at any time, so if she is tonight, I'll drive her home."

"Sounds good, son. See you soon."

After they left, Marcus pulled his chair closer to my bed, and we started chatting again.

"I feel bad that Allan and I aren't hitting off immediately like the rest of us have." I admitted, my face falling.

"Look, Becks was the cutest sister we could have ever asked for." Marcus told me. His voice was heavy with depression, but he was smiling at the fond memories that were obviously coming to mind. "Her optimism and her ability to talk to anybody made her a great sibling. Despite her being in the surf club, she never really considered anyone her best friend. That is, until *you* came along."

"Thanks, Marcus, that...that really makes me feel good." I said, tears coming into my eyes again.

"And don't worry about Allan." Marcus continued. "He's still devastated by the loss of his sister. Becky was one of the few young people that liked him for the longest part of his life, and now she's gone, before he got to see her graduate high school. Give him time, and he'll eventually like you."

"I hope so."

Just then, the nurse on duty came toward my bed with a smile on her face. Her name was Sandra and was very friendly. Her blonde hair was streaked with turquoise highlights, and her gray eyes sparkled as she looked at me. "Well, Nicole, according to this morning's x-rays and MRIs, you are in good enough health for you to leave."

"Really?" I asked, finally feeling fully happy.

"Really, really!" Sandra said, grinning. "I believe your brother here can drive you home, so you may leave whenever you feel like it. Have a nice night!"

As we began packing up, something came to me. "What of my belongings at mine and my Dad's home? We may not have a lot, but I still have to get it from there to your guys' place."

"Way ahead of you." Marcus assured me. "As soon as Mom and Dad officially adopted you, the boys and I had permission to enter your house, using a set of keys found with your dad. All of the stuff is either in a storage container on our driveway or in the house. What we confirmed to be your stuff has been moved into Becky's old room."

"I'll have to give away a lot." I said quietly, standing up from my bed and reaching for a backpack Anthony had brought for me the night before. After putting on a pair of socks, I shouldered my bag on my good arm. "Most of my dad's stuff is useless to me."

"Well, you still have a few days off, so you'll have time to go through it." Marcus told me. "Let's go home."

"But what about the hospital bill?" I said, just as we passed the triage desk.

"Mom had the hospital charge it to our insurance." Marcus patted my shoulder. "Plus, a GoFundMe page helped out the survivors. Over eighty thousand dollars has been raised already."

"Wow, awesome."

"Not to worry, everything has been taken care of."

***

It turned out that the Millers lived in La Jolla, a long way away from the neighbourhood Dad and I had lived in. As we parked across the street from the home, I got my first look at where Becky came from, and I was stunned. The house was huge, with white and umber plaster outer walls and red terracotta shingles. It faced out onto the ocean, with a beautiful view of the Pacific and palm trees. A four-car garage sat at the back of an equally massive driveway. A half-sized shipping container sat on one side of the drive-way, just as Marcus had said. As I looked up at the house in utter disbelief, I could not believe that I was now living here. I found myself thinking, '*what the* heck *was Becky* doing *at Lincoln High School?*'

Reading my face, Marcus chuckled. "I know what you're thinking. What is a rich girl doing at places like Lincoln High School and working a job like a diner waitress, huh?"

Blushing to the roots of my hair, I squeaked, "Something like that."

"Well, my parents raised us under the idea that we shouldn't flaunt our wealth." Marcus explained. Locking his car, he walked me up to the house. "Which is why we all have had jobs of our own, and why Becky never went into depth about our family. We are *technically* supposed to be going to La Jolla High School, but Mom and Dad wanted us to go to a school that they thought would gain us a better, fairer life. So, they heard of Lincoln's reputation, and we've been going there ever since. Not to mention, Mom and Dad preferred to send us to public school than to a snobby private school, and, quite frankly, I have to agree with them."

Nodding, I contemplated what I was just told. All the while, Marcus was fumbling with his keys. As he opened the front door, he finished by saying, "Welcome home, sister."

Stepping inside, I looked around and saw that the Millers were indeed modest. The décor was simple, and the furniture designs were ones found more at Ikea than at Grayson. Nevertheless, it still didn't hide the fact that the place was, like, *three times* the size of my old house. As I put my back-pack down and undid my shoes, my new parents walked up. Though I was familiar with them, I couldn't help but feel like I was being reintroduced to them.

"Ah, you're home. Perfect!" My new dad said excitedly. His hair was a dark coppery tone, streaked with gray. His tawny eyes were bright, and his build was one of a farmer gone slightly to seed. As he came up and hugged me, his tone turned gentle. "How are you feeling?"

"Better, thanks." I whispered, smiling.

"Well, as you recall, my name is Jameson, but you can call me Dad or Jamie if you want."

"I think Jamie will be okay." I said quietly, trying hard not to think of my actual dad. "Sorry."

"No, we understand." Theresa stated. She was wearing way more casual clothes than what I had seen her in thus far. She had changed from the work clothes she had on at the hospital and now had on a simple pink blouse and black yoga pants, furthering her appearance as an older version of Becky. "Looks like if we had stuck around for a little bit more, we could've driven you home ourselves!"

"No prob, Theresa." I replied, taking my windbreaker off. "You didn't know."

"Well, we just sat down for supper. Right this way!" Jamie announced.

As I ate a delicious meal of spaghetti and meatballs, I got a feel for the house's atmosphere. The family was tight knit, despite the parents being workaholics and Marcus and Samuel living out of the house. The twins countered this by frequently coming by to visit with their families. Anthony and Allan still lived in the house to help save money for their college tuition and occupied two side-by-side rooms in the basement. Jamie and Theresa shared a massive master bedroom on the second floor, adjacent to their shared office. My room was also upstairs, and that meant I had a bathroom to myself.

During dessert, I found out that there were two cats in the house. One was a gray one named Moon and the other a pure-white one named Jack. They were eating beside us at the table, and when I was introduced to them, I reached over and scratched Jack. I was also told that Becky had kept a fish tank in her room, which had three goldfish in it, named Goldie, Arnold, and Phelps.

"I'll look after the fish." Allan volunteered. "I've been doing it since...well...the incident, so I know how."

"Thanks, Allan, but I think I'll handle that." I declined, rubbing Moon's belly now. "I've never had a pet in my life, so I'm stoked to now have five!"

"Please, Nicole, can we at least partner up?"

Glancing over, I noticed that Allan was looking at me with an expression that I never expected, desperation. I sat up and realized he was pleading for something to keep himself connected to his late sister, so I said, "Okay. We can alternate weeks in charge. Just make sure to knock before coming into my room."

Chuckling, a weak smile appeared on Allan's face. "Agreed, my sister."

As the realization of Allan at least recognizing me as his sister hit me, I decided to change the subject. I began talking with my new guardians, and I found out that Jamie and Theresa worked hard all day, with Theresa playing her role as a lawyer and Jamie working as the owner of a prominent commercial real estate company. Though the parents were absent for a great amount of the day, the kids still got to see them. This reminded me so much of my dad, I didn't mind it at all.

I further discovered that, as I was a longer way away from school than what I used to be, I would have to take the bus to get to school and to work, which was a change that, for once, worried me.

"I'm going to have to look carefully at the bus schedule to see what I'll be taking, when I'll be taking it, and where I'll be picked up."

"Don't worry, you take the same bus we do." Anthony assured me, waving his forkful of pie. "We'll show you in a few days how to get to Lincoln."

"Thanks, Anthony."

"Call me, Tony, sis." He grinned, touching my hand with his. "We all have nicknames. Marcus is Marky, Samuel is Sammy, and Allan is, obviously, Al."

I quickly looked over at Allan and asked, "Do you mind if I call you Al?"

Contemplating it for a second, he replied with, "No, I don't mind. Would you mind if we called you Nicky?"

After thinking about it, I said, "Yes, I would mind. That name died with my dad. Nick, I wouldn't mind."

"Very well, Nick it is." Jamie declared, standing up and gathering our dishes.

As dinner was cleared out, I made my way upstairs with my backpack to see my new room. As I fully opened the ajar door, I saw a clean, tidy bedroom decorated with posters and pictures. The walls were painted a lovely light-yellow colour, and it made the room feel warm and welcoming. The bed was double-sized, with a plethora of stuffed animals on it. As I walked in, I also saw that Moon was asleep on the bed, and I quickly went over and scratched her behind her ears.

The room's window was right above the bed, and it looked out directly onto the ocean; I looked out onto the view as I petted Moon. Straightening up and dropping my bag on the floor, I glanced around further. Across the room from the closet and the bed was the fish tank sitting on the dresser, and I decided to look closely into the water.

Watching the fish for a few minutes, I noticed that they were constantly swimming up to the surface and then sinking back down. Catching on, I looked around and saw that Allan had left a feeding schedule taped to the side of the tank with a can of food. Reading the schedule, I saw it was in fact time for a feeding, and I read the can to figure out how to feed them. After I dropped some food in the tank for the fish, I looked over the dresser, which was long and had a large mirror in its centre.

In front of that mirror, a colourful picture frame stood alone, and the photo within was of me and Becky at the beach. I recognized it as one taken on Becky's phone by Colby on my first night in the Surf Club. I knew that because Becky had sent me a copy on my phone. My emotions were mixed as I picked up the frame and sat down on the bed. I looked around and realized that I was now in Becky's world and should honour it. I put the photo down and looked in the closet, seeing a lot of empty space. While I thought of how I was going to organize my clothes, someone knocked on the door. Turning towards the door, I saw that Theresa had followed me from the dining room, a pair of mugs in her hands.

"Want some tea?" She inquired. "It's camomile. Good for soothing pain."

"Thanks." I replied, watching as Theresa walked in.

Pacing around the room silently for a few seconds, she asked quietly, "Like it?"

"I...I don't know what to think." I said, looking around. "The bed is comfy, the closet looks good, and the view is perfect. But it still feels like I shouldn't be here. Becky should be here with me."

Sympathy filled Theresa's eyes. "Don't worry, Nick. She'd be happy to share her room with you."

"I know." I replied. "I plan to keep the décor the same. I won't ever take stuff down and I'll try and keep Becky's memory alive."

Sitting down on the bed, Theresa looked around her late daughter's room. She sighed and nodded. "I think that is a perfect idea."

I sat beside her, and finally began feeling at home. "I think I can say this at last. Thank-you for all of this."

"You're welcome," Theresa said, hugging me as we leaned our heads against each other, "my daughter."

{ **8** }

I Set My Sights on a New Life

The next week was a blur. I quickly settled into my new home and began sorting through the stuff recovered by my brothers. Luckily, my dad and I were extremely conservative and didn't have much stuff, so it didn't take long. As I emptied the container and filled up my new closet and dresser, I began to make Becky's old room more my own. Though I kept the posters and the pictures up, I changed a few things, so the room was more comfortable for me.

My first weekend with the Millers was the first time that I felt happy since the shooting. Problem was though, the weekend would also be my final days at home alone, as I was expected back at school that following Monday. Therefore, I decided to make it count.

Saturday was a day spent cleaning the house, and the boys had a fun way of doing this. They treated each room like an old-fashioned movie car wash and cleaned them like they were women in bikinis. It was hilarious to watch, and I loved helping them (disclaimer: no bikinis were involved in the cleaning of this house).

After the house was clean, I began to experience my first hiccups with the family. As we had lunch, I was enjoying an egg-salad sandwich when I said something I quickly regretted.

"Shit, this homemade bread is fucking delicious!" I said, my rebellious side finally coming out. I had begun to loosen up a little since arriving at Lincoln, and my language control had gotten a little lax as of late.

In response, Anthony and Allan looked at me in stunned silence, and Theresa quietly gasped and frowned. Jamie, who was reading the Saturday newspaper, told me, "Becky, that's two quarters in the swear jar! You know the rules!"

That remark made the scene about a thousand times worse. Feeling like someone had just punched me in the gut, I looked towards my new dad. "Um, Jamie, I'm Nicole."

Dropping his paper in shock, he appeared mortified. "Oh, right, sorry, Nicole. Anyway, we have a strict no-swearing policy here, and if you do swear, it's a quarter in the swear jar, which is underneath the microwave."

"Okay." I said, pulling change out of my pocket and making my deposit. I felt awful that I had said those things, not to mention I felt a little saddened to know that my new family was still having a hard time adjusting to having me, and not Becky, in their midst.

***

After finishing my food, I made my way down to the beach to surf. It felt terrible to do it without Colby or Becky, and when I arrived, the surf club was already there.

"Nicole!" Pablo shouted, looking up from polishing his board, which was coloured like the Mexican flag. He seemed very surprised to see me there. "*Mi amiga*, it is *fantástico* to see you!"

"Same to you, Pablo." I said, clapping him on his shoulder.

As Sam walked up to me, she hugged me once again. As we both stared out to the beautiful ocean scene, Sam said, "Just not the same without them, is it?"

Sighing, I nodded. "Indeed, it's not."

We then waded out and surfed for a while, but we soon discovered our lack of enthusiasm for the activity, not to mention it was also hard for me as I still had my arm in a sling for my shoulder. So, combining those reasons, we came back onto the beach. Sitting down on Sam's blanket, we talked back and forth, catching up with each other on what had happened since I was released; I was curious to hear what was going on at the school.

"The principal cancelled classes after the shooting. The only thing to do for us at school were talking with grief councellors." Sam told me, her knees pulled up to her chest and her arms wrapped around them.

"Yeah, I got visited by those a few times while in hospital." I said, bringing my knees up to my chest as well. "They do help, but they don't really give a direction to go to if you've lost a close loved one."

"Can't say I disagree with you." Sam said, nibbling on a Fruit-by-the-Foot she had in her picnic basket. "My parents were nearly hit that night, and it shook me up quite badly. All I gotta say is, I don't ever want to go through that again."

"Same." I replied, pulling out an apple from the basket.

After a brief pause for contemplation, I brought up something that had been on my mind since I woke up in hospital.

"Sam, do you ever get the feeling that things in life, both good and bad, are meant to happen?" I asked, my voice shaking a little.

Looking at me carefully, Sam replied, "I guess. I mean, we all have a destiny, don't we? It's The Lord's will that decides what will happen in our lives. And He's not always kind."

"Well, maybe this whole thing is a sign of what my destiny is supposed to be." I continued, my voice steadying and getting stronger. "I think my destiny is to end gun violence in this country."

"You may think that, but so do over eighty-five million *other* people in this nation." Sam pointed out, rolling her eyes. "What are you getting at, Nick?"

"What I'm saying is that maybe those people haven't been able to make much progress because they haven't had the proper leader come forward yet."

"And let me guess, *you* want to be that leader?" Sam responded, raising one eyebrow.

"Essentially, yes. I feel that, with the navy, and by extension the whole military, backing me up, I have a prime opportunity to join the ranks of those fighting against things like the Second Amendment and those nitwits in the N.R.A.

Not to mention, my new mom has agreed to aid me in any legal battle I become a part of. Combine all that, and the fact that a high-ranking military officer has now been shot due to this violence, I think that our voices will finally be heard and be able to garner some control of guns in this country."

"It'll never work, my friend." Sam told me, shaking her head. "Even if you halt the sales of guns, as easy as they are, gunmen will still get their firearms from places like Mexico or the black market overseas. It's impossible to stem the tide completely."

"I'm not looking to stem the tide completely." I admitted, turning up my palms. "I know that will be impossible. What I *do* want to do is restrict the ability for people to *get* firearms and install a much better way to track them. In other words, make it so that the easiest way *to* get guns *is* to get them from the black market. Plus, I want to make it so that the only times you can carry a gun are either if you're a cop or a hunter."

"There's no way Capitol Hill is going to do away with the Second Amendment entirely." Sam countered. "Those old codgers will never let it die."

"Then we amend the Amendment!" I said forcefully, my emotions running high and in a new direction all of a sudden. "We make it so that the only time Americans have the right to bear arms is when the nation is under direct attack. And I don't mean those frilly little terrorist bombers, I mean when some great entity begins firing upon our military bases and challenging us directly within our borders."

"But..." Sam began, clearly trying to find a new angle.

"There are no buts, Sam!" I snapped, shutting her down and slamming my right fist into my left palm. "This is a disagreement that has reached critical boiling point here. To me, it is America's new Civil War. The two sides are pro- and anti-gun fighters. More people will needlessly die if nothing is done. Whether it's at a school, a church, or soon even maybe a mall, these gunners will find some sort of reason or vendetta against someone or some*thing* and go charging into public, all guns blazing. I seek to stop that, so no one has to suffer like I have."

After pausing for a second, I finished in a much quieter, quivering tone. "It's what my dad would have wanted."

Sam was speechless after my little rant. She stared at me in complete shock for a long while. After nearly ten minutes, she finally spoke up. "I...I am impressed. I guess this is where all your grief was channelled into. What you just said has given me a new perspective on the whole gun crisis in our country. It also showed a side of Nicole Miller that I've never seen before! When you set your mind on something, you *really* focus on it and are determined to see it through. *Wow.*"

Smiling, I looked at my friend and said, "That's my dad for you. He taught me that giving up gets you nowhere, so when you set your goals, make a plan to see them through. And boy do I have a plan."

"Oh, you do, do you? I guess this is the part where you tell me your master plan to change the world's most stubborn democracy by yourself?" Sam asked, smirking.

"Change? Yes. By myself? No." I clarified. "The first part

of my 'master plan' is to start an advocacy group with my friends and anybody at school willing to listen so I can create a louder voice about our plight. Then, we'll start connecting with similar groups around the county, state, and eventually the nation until our collective voice is loud enough to march on Capitol Hill and make our demands known. Besides, with the military on our side and a legal backer, I have some heavy artillery as back up."

"Are you sure the military will *want* this to happen?" Sam inquired, offering me a Popsicle from her cooler. "I mean, many of those brutes are who's *causing* the problem."

"Watch who you're calling brutes." I warned in a dangerously calm voice, glaring at Sam. "Anyway, I know it sounds like a long shot, but I've been on enough military bases to know that it's really the hillbillies, wackos, and so-called 'gun enthusiasts' that really are the advocates for the keeping of the status quo. The military forces are *against* it. They want change. They want things harder for civilians to get their weapons, and they've been trying to get their senior officers to hear sense. Now that one of said officers is dead because of mass-shootings, a stronger plea will definitely be going out. Now's our chance to fight."

Sam suddenly stood up and motioned that I follow. When I did, she hugged me strongly and then held my shoulders, careful not to jostle my hurt one. I looked into her eyes and saw tears, but she was smiling at the same time. "There's only one thing I have to say in response to that. Where do I sign up?"

Those last five words warmed my heart. I embraced my

friend again and stared back out at the beach, this time in a more hopeful mood. "Well, if we want our voices to get heard, we've got work to do."

{ **9** }

They Came From Miles Around

My first day back was a day of sympathy for me. The school had been closed the whole time I was gone, so this was a first day back for everybody, and no matter where I went, almost everyone was giving me condolences and pats on the back. This suited me fine, as I knew those who felt sympathy for me were potential members for my advocacy. The daily announcements began with two minutes of silence as we remembered those who had died. The number had apparently increased to forty the night before due to some of those severely injured having died from complications from their injuries. This galvanized my push and made me even more determined to get my group started.

The theatre was still closed off as a crime scene, so we had drama class in the gym. Gym class was usually outside anyways, so this didn't bother Coach Saunders much at all. There was still a police presence hanging around the auditorium, as well as an armed guard in the lunchroom when noontime came around. Where there were once laid-back surfers and pumped-up athletes were now Kevlar-jacketed riflemen and a highly tense atmosphere. It was as if my school was holding its collective breath, waiting for a second attack.

As I walked through the cafeteria with my tray, I had a flashback to the spaghetti day when I first met my now-deceased friends. The memory made me feel depressed. As I sat down with some of my surfer-friends and Sam, who was now a full member of the Surf Club, I couldn't help but notice that everyone's eyes were on me again. I also heard whispers from people around me, but only snippets.

"She's the crazy one the cops wanted to see." One voice said quietly.

"So, you don't believe her story of being a hero?" Another replied.

"Puh-lease! She's just trying to get attention!" The first answered, laughing.

As my anger fired up, I turned around to try and find the speakers, but I failed to do so. As I returned to eating, more voices were coming to my ears.

"There's No-Hits Nicole!" A third speaker breathed to friend as they walked by. "She's a real-life Supergirl! She's practically bullet-proof!"

I continued to try and follow the trail of the conversations, but it was impossible. It was then that I decided to join in the loud conversation coming from my own table. Sam was engaged in a lively argument with Frankie over the latest episode of Survivor, a show all of us were immersed in.

"Isn't it *obvious*? Annie should have been voted off!" Sam said, slamming her fist on the table. "She just managed to swindle the votes away from her and on to Chris!"

"No way!" Frankie replied, waving his hands. "She was just playing the game! That's how Survivor works for villains!"

"But she doesn't *do* anything around camp! The only reason she's lasted *this long* is her swindling!"

"Yeah, but-"

"If I may interject." I said professionally, raising a finger. When I looked up from my enchiladas, I tried hard not to laugh at the faces my friends were giving me. "You both bring up very good points. Annie should have been voted off for her inability to help in challenges and around camp, but her social methods are getting her respect in certain people in her tribe. She probably won't last long if she keeps yapping her mouth off like she did last tribal, but I could be wrong. Don't you guys agree?"

My pair of friends were staring at me for a while, then thought about it for a second, then they looked at each other, stunned, and nodded in unison. That did it for me; I burst out laughing.

"You guys look *hilarious*!" I screamed, my laughs echoing around the room like a foreign language.

Catching on, Frankie began chuckling too. "I guess we were pretty stupefied. We weren't expecting such a response from you, I guess."

"Hey, a girl's gotta have *something* to watch and keep her entertained while in hospital." I said, raising an eyebrow. "I've been keeping up with Survivor this whole time."

"No, we just weren't expecting it *today.*" Frankie pointed out. "It being our first day back and all. We'd thought you'd be a little more interested in the, um, surround sound."

"Meh." I shrugged. "I don't care what the others are thinking."

"Dudette, they're calling you No-Hits Nicole!" Tommy told me, jumping into our conversation from beside Frankie. Tommy was your quintessential California surfer-dude, with a laid-back attitude that rivalled Colby's. "How could you not love that?"

"Well, right off the hopper, I *was* hit." I said, patting my sling. "Secondly, these titles mean nothing to me unless they can help me accomplish my goal."

"Oh, and what goal is that?" Jeff asked, stealing a fry from Sam's plate; the two of them had started dating right after the shooting as a means of comforting each other, and were sitting side-by-side.

"Starting an advocacy group to end mass-shootings." I said simply, making it sound like it was obvious. "I have the opportunity and the professional backers. Now, I just need the numbers. Sam has already agreed to sign up. Can I count on you guys to join?"

"Um, do you have the principal's permission?" Jeff asked, frowning. "If you want the group to participate in the school and have support of the school, you need her permission first."

"Oh." I stated, my shoulders slumping. "Didn't think of that."

"Don't worry, my friend." Frankie assured me. "We'll be

behind you the whole way. Besides, the principal will be more than willing to help out, after what you did."

"I'm not so sure." Jeff said uncertainly. "I've heard she's been a Nazi when it comes to the extra-curriculars over the years, so I'd be careful with how you position yourself."

"What do you mean?" I asked, curious. "Wouldn't she love to see students interested in clubs outside of school?"

Laughing once without humour, Jeff continued. "You'd think so, but no. I almost had to beg her to keep the robotics club together after we lost state championships last year. She looks for very specific things in a club, and when we didn't bring home gold for her, she almost revoked our ability to be a club."

"In other words, make sure how you describe the advocacy group is something the school needs." Frankie summarized.

"If you say so. I'll go to her after I'm done eating my lunch here."

And when that happened, about a half-hour later, I was standing outside the office, waiting for the administrators to open the doors. When the one on duty came by, I walked in and knocked on the door for the principal's office. After being buzzed in, I presented myself before the principal, Mrs. Randall.

"Well, Ms. Miller, this is a pleasant surprise." She announced, indicating for me to sit. "What can I do for our school's mighty hero?"

After sitting down, I got right down to business. "I was recently informed that I need your permission to begin a school group from scratch, so I am here to ask for such permission."

"What group may that be, Nicole?" Mrs. Randall asked, resting her chin on the top of her hands. Her winged glasses glittered in the light filtering through the window, which also lit up her graying blonde hair.

"That group is one of advocates and promotes the end of mass-shootings and the stronger control of guns in this fair nation of ours. I feel it is something our school needs."

A look of complete and utter satisfaction spread across the principal's face. "Well, I was wondering when this was coming. Though I do have to say that what happened at our musical was absolutely heart-wrenching, I cannot say that your group would be able to do much to change the status quo in the U.S. I'm afraid I can't give you permission to form that group, as I see no real sport, cultural, or educational outcome for it."

Complete shock and disbelief hit me. I kept my composure, but my mind was quickly filling with anger. "Mrs. Randall, as I am hoping you are aware, there are many of these groups across the country, even in this very *county*! I cannot see why you believe this group has no educational outcome! We want to bring awareness to a serious problem in America! This *is* an educational group!"

"Nevertheless, I cannot see why this group would do anything besides constantly reminding our students of the horrors and trauma that they went through. If they need help coping, we have guidance counsellors for that." Mrs. Randall said, the tone in her voice turning smug. "This meeting is over. Now, you best get to class, or you'll be late."

As I stood up and walked to the door, I thought of something. As I touched the doorknob, I turned around and asked the principal, "Mrs. Randall, do you own a gun yourself?"

A look of surprise soured the satisfaction on the principal's face. "Well, yes, actually."

"That's all I needed to hear." I nodded, walking out in a huff.

***

That night, I described my group's status, or lack thereof, to my family at supper.

"Well, the principal won't let my group begin, because she 'doesn't see any sport, cultural, or educational outcome for it'." I explained bitterly, raising air quotes.

Jamie cried out a loud curse in response, clearly showing he was angry beyond belief.

"Honey, a quarter into the swear jar, please." Theresa said sternly. "What your dad is trying to say is that your principal was wrong. Your group is totally legitimate; she just doesn't want you to stir up the waters."

"Yeah, but she has final say over the groups that occupy her school. If she says no, it doesn't happen."

"But what if you went over her head?" Anthony asked slyly. "There are people that supersede her."

"You mean, the board of education?" I asked, suddenly intrigued.

"Exactly!" Allan stated. He had been warming up to me more and more each day, and he suddenly seemed a lot nicer to me today than most. "Marky and Sammy were so notorious at school, that the current superintendent knows our family! They-"

"Allan!" Jamie snapped. "Sorry, Nick, your brother likes to exaggerate. Your twin brothers were troublemakers, yes, but we already knew the superintendent before they went to school. His wife has been a colleague of mine for years, and we talk nearly every day. We can arrange for you to get an interview with the superintendent without much hassle."

I experienced the second wave of shock of the day. "You guys would do that for me?"

"Of course." Jamie stated. "You are our heroic daughter, and we will do anything to help you. If ending this violence once and for all is what your goal is, then we will pull out all the stops for you."

I leapt up and hugged my new parents. "You guys are *AWESOME!*"

***

The next few days were ones of patience for me. I still had no official group, but using Facebook, I managed to garner a solid following amongst my friends and classmates. I also convinced them that, when I travelled to the board of education, they should join me as a sign of solidarity and the idea's strength.

The night after our conversation, Jamie came home and told us that his colleague, named Beverley Horner, would indeed speak to her husband Bruce and arrange a time for me to speak to him. I was eternally grateful for their help and felt like nothing could stop me.

When I was at school, I had a smug feeling in my head every time I looked at Mrs. Randall. My friends and I were starting to get excited over the fact that our group would soon be able to start raising awareness of our belief. The teachers seemed to get wind of what we were planning, and they seemed to favour our side. Coach Saunders let me be the captain of one of our basketball teams during gym class, right out of the blue, while he decided Sam to be the other captain. He also let me choose first, giving me the best play-ers for the day's game. My math teacher, Mr. McCoy, gave me a hint-filled cheat-sheet to study with for the upcoming exam, and when I questioned him about it, he said, "Just in case."

I was surprised by the reaction I was getting from the staff, but it still gave me even more reason to fight for my cause. By the time I got the news that I had an interview with Bruce, I had gained a following of over ten thousand on Facebook, and that was just from my school. When I called out to my old friends on the bases and garnered a further six hundred. I knew that, when I showed these numbers to Bruce and the rest of the board, there would be no doubt that this group had a reason to exist offline. Little did I realize that the numbers I had then were just the tip of the oncoming iceberg.

{ **10** }

I Begin My Fight

Ten days after my return to school, I was still experiencing nightmares about the shooting. Though I didn't tell anyone about them, they still scared me, but they were constantly reminding me that I had been too slow to save my friends and dad. This drove me to ensure no one ever had to go through this again, and my campaign began to rise. It was then that I ran into my second major obstacle in my fight to end gun violence. And boy, was this one ever a doozy.

After I got off of school, I was sitting on the beach, doing homework and enjoying the sun. When I finished my assignments for the day, I decided to look at my group's Facebook page. Laura's dad offered free Wi-Fi to the beach, so the Internet was not a problem, but when I got onto the page, I found out something weird.

"That's funny." I stated, frowning.

"What is?" Sam asked. She was typing an essay on her laptop beside me, and she didn't look up from her screen.

"I can't edit anything on the Facebook page. I wanted

to check on whether we had gotten any new members and change the day when our first meeting was going to be. But now, I can't."

"Let me look." Sam said, setting her laptop aside.

Passing on my laptop, I began to feel really concerned. As I read the words that were on the page, I realized that they weren't the ones I had put on the page earlier that morning. In fact, the words were describing us as a group that was actually planning *more* mass-shootings, not to end them.

"Uh, oh." Same said simply, looking worried. "I think you've been hacked, Nick."

"Really? How?" I asked, feeling quite surprised.

"Someone must have seen our page and decided to try and ruin us. This is not good."

"No kidding." I said. I then looked at the followers' counter, and suddenly, the numbers began falling, first one-by-one, then by the tens. We had been nearing eleven thousand the previous day, but now the number was rapidly dropping past nine thousand.

"No!" I yelled, shaking my computer. "No, guys, don't leave! This isn't my doing!"

"What's wrong now?" Sam asked, a slight hint of panic in her voice.

"People are unfollowing our group! We're losing our followers!"

"And look at the comments!" Sam pointed out. "'You guys led me to believe you were trying to end gun violence. But now I see you were lying the whole time! See ya!'"

"What can we do?" I asked, my voice really panicky now.

"Shut down the page and call Facebook. They always tell you to report hacks."

"Okay, let's do it." I pulled out my phone. As I unlocked it, I saw that I had about a billion emails flooding my inbox, and when I checked it out, I saw that they were all hate mail from our supporters.

"People are emailing me too! Mean emails! We've crashed!"

"Forget that for now!" Sam shot, putting her laptop away. "Call Facebook and report this hacking R.F.N.!"

As I dialled the help number, I talked with a rep, and they guided me through the process of freezing my account and fixing the problem. As I got off the phone, I was reeling from what just happened.

"What now? It's gonna be impossible to recover from this." Sam asked delicately.

"What, you think I'm stopping at this hurdle," I told her defiantly. "after all that's happened? No, this may be a major set-back, but those who have a bit of logic should be able to be swayed again. We just need to find out who did this."

"Well, Facebook might be able to figure that out for you." Sam agreed.

All of a sudden, my phone rang out. It was Theresa.

"Theresa, what's up?"

"You've been summoned to the school board." She told me. "Now. And this isn't for a simple interview. The whole school board wants to talk to you."

"What?" I shouted, taken aback.

"Allan is on his way to pick you up with a change of clothes, so get ready!"

"You got it, Mom!" I said, standing up quickly and packing up.

"What's going on?" Sam asked, raising one eyebrow.

"The school board wants to see me, like, tonight." I told her. "And when I say the school board, I mean the *whole* school board, not just the superintendent."

"Really? Wow!"

"Wait, this might be the way I regain my support." I told her, a lightbulb going off in my mind. "Get everybody on the phone. Call up everyone you can and get them down to the school board. This probably will be how I save myself."

"You got it." Sam responded, also standing up. "See you soon."

Allan arrived in ten minutes, and I changed at the surf shop. I then raced to Allan's car, which was a Cadillac, and I was panting. As we peeled off from the curb, I was trying my hardest to formulate a speech for my meeting.

"Don't worry, sis!" Allan said, sitting in the drivers' seat. Anthony, Samuel and Marcus were with us, while our parents were riding to the board of education in Jamie's Lincoln. "Everything will be fine!"

"I'm not worried, Al. I'm just concerned that my group will be stuck as no more than an online chatroom. Not that that will halt my efforts, just hinder them."

"Well, there's only one way for you to find out!" Marcus encouraged.

"I suppose." I said. I remained quiet the rest of our trip to the board as I tried to figure out what I was going to say. Luckily, I had been practicing a little bit in front of my mirror, so I had gotten better at public speaking. When we arrived, I had a pretty good idea of what I was going to say.

"Well, go on! We'll be watching!" Samuel prompted.

"Okay, guys. See you soon!"

As I walked into the building, I was met by a guard and she guided me to my meeting. I was being led to the meeting theatre, and I realized that this would be the first breaking point for my fight; if I failed here, I never would be able to rise up like I wanted. So, understandably, I was on pins and needles as I heard loud voices coming from within the room.

"Right through here." The guard said, motioning me through the door.

As I stepped into the room, I saw that, yes, the entire school board was present, as well as Mrs. Randall. As I walked across the theatre, I heard talking coming from above me, and when I looked up, I saw a viewing deck, with my family and many of my online members sitting down. I realized that I would indeed have some back-up, and this strengthened my resolve.

"Sit right here, Ms. Miller." Bruce told me, indicating a seat and table next to Mrs. Randall. When I sat down as requested, he continued. "Alright, now that everyone is present and prepared, we can get down to business. I have called this special meeting of the board for the San Diego Unified School District to discuss a matter that has come to our attention and has generated great controversy across our city. That matter is the subject of creating an advocacy group at Lincoln High School on the topic of gun violence.

"This group's existence has been thwarted by the principal

of the school, despite the catastrophe the school just had to endure as a result of said gun violence. We are here to discuss the reasons for this rejection. Chelsea Randall, principal of Lincoln High School, you will state your case first, then Nicole Miller will present hers. Principal Randall, the podium is yours."

Looking like she was facing down an escaped tiger, Mrs. Randall stood up and began speaking, reading off of a paper in front of her. "Thank you, Mr. Horner. As I have already described to Ms. Miller here when she came to my office, I cannot see any cultural or educational benefit or outcome from creating this group. On top of that, I believe that the group would be a constant reminder of the incident when many of my students would love to forget it.

"This group, I believe, would be a terrible mistake for the school community, as it is still reeling from the loss. If Ms. Miller here were to be allowed to lead her campaign, she would be a continuation of the despair, hardship, and depression our school is so desperately trying to recover from as we speak."

Taking a breath and looking more confident, Mrs. Randall continued. "Therefore, it is my stance to prevent the creation of the group in order to keep the atmosphere in my school calm and collective, as well as to prevent school-wide disagreements and fights between those who are for and those who are against stricter gun laws. In fact, I am even hearing today that Ms. Miller's Facebook page is stating her *true* intentions. These points are what I am standing upon and I hope you guys see my point of view."

As Mrs. Randall sat down, I couldn't help but feel angry, nearly outraged about her reasoning. Taking a deep breath, I stood up at Bruce's request and began my own speech. I don't know where the words came from, but they suddenly appeared in my mind.

"Good evening, board members, Mrs. Randall, and distinguished guests. Ever since the tragic incident that occurred at my high school, I have been trying to find a way to channel my raw emotions. I decided to do so by vouching to end gun attacks like the one I was a victim of. Though I have managed to gain a significant following in and around the school, I have been unable to officially create the group I desire due to our principal's narrow-minded views about the subject.

"As she just stated, she thinks the group will continue the pain students are feeling about the incident, whereas I feel the group will give those feeling that pain a conduit and a place to focus the pain instead of bottling it up. The counselling the school has provided only goes so far, and only lasts so long. I feel my group will give the students that need a voice a way to speak out, and a means to vent their emotions.

"For the part that Mrs. Randall described as there being potential conflict, I doubt anyone at Lincoln will disagree with us after what has happened at the school. In fact, the only person I feel that will be against us if this group is created is Mrs. Randall herself. She stated to me directly at the end of our meeting that she owns guns herself.

"I feel this shows that, if she is preventing us from forming the group, she is only doing it out of personal interest, and is contributing to the problem my followers are trying to end. Also, the Facebook page Mrs. Randall is referring to is actually the victim of a hack by a so-far unknown assailant. Our views are *anti-gun* and will forever remain so.

"In conclusion, school board members, I, Nicole Miller, tried to stop the gunman from causing any harm to our school, but failed. I feel this is my way to redeem myself and become the hero my classmates are advertising me as."

As I sat down the viewing balcony exploded into applause. I looked over at Mrs. Randall, whose face was contorted in absolute rage, and I smiled. I knew I had just pissed off a woman of power, but it wasn't my first time. Though my dad was an officer at the naval bases, he and I rarely got to see each other most of the time, so when I was younger, I used, um, *various* methods to get attention, including acts that drew the ire of many of my handlers. So, when I saw that look on Mrs. Randall, I didn't feel at all concerned.

"You're lying." Mrs. Randall whispered to me. "The school will fall into chaos if your group is created. And your Facebook gathering won't last long either."

"We'll see." I breathed back. Something then came to mind. "Wait, how did you know about the Facebook group?"

"Oh, come on, you think you're the only one who operates behind closed doors?" She smiled slyly. She then leaned back with her arms behind her head.

I shot to my feet quickly and stated. "I'm sorry to interrupt, Mr. Horner, but I have something to add."

Silence came to the room. "What is that, Ms. Miller?" A surprised Mr. Horner inquired.

"As stated before, earlier today, my Facebook followers were misled to believe that my group's true intention was to plan more attacks, not to end them. This has torpedoed my follower list, and I now feel I know who hacked my group's page: Mrs. Randall herself. She was the first to mention something about Facebook, and I knew that only someone involved with this would know about our new issue. So, I'm adding in the accusation that Mrs. Randall hacked our account to kill my support group."

Shocked silence pervaded after I sat back down again. Mrs. Randall looked like I had just slapped her, and she looked even more outraged, if that was at all possible. She then shot to her own feet. "Mr. Horner! You cannot possibly believe this outrageous accusation!"

"What Ms. Miller has stated is indeed incredulous. However, your apparent deep knowledge of the group's falling numbers and change of motives when Ms. Miller had not mentioned them prior are quite suspicious. We will now deliberate all that has been said."

As the board resumed their talking, the crowd in the viewer's box erupted in outrage. The noise became so loud that Bruce Horner called for quiet and had to use a microphone to gain attention. After a few further minutes of deliberation, the board called us to attention.

"After much, very deep discussion, the five of us have come to a consensus. The gun-laws advocacy group will indeed be allowed to go through. The evidence provided here shows that Principal Randall had no grounds to deny the group's existence in the first place and will not have any grounds to deny them in the future. As well, she has committed an ethical crime that violates our school board policies. Thus, the advocacy group will go through."

A roar of cheers and applause came from the viewing gallery, and Bruce let it go for a few seconds before he called for silence. When the room fell quiet again, he continued. "On that note, we have also made the decision to demote Principal Randall back to her previous position of history teacher at Lincoln High School, while Victor Van Der Hoof will take over her position."

"*Excuse* me?" Mrs. Randall shrieked, shooting to her feet again. She looked like Bruce had *also* hit her, and her face was contorted in scandalized fury.

"You're excused, Chelsea." Bruce said gently, but firmly. "Our decision was not only due to the policy violation, but also due to the unfair and unnecessary restrictions you have been instilling in several groups at your school the entire time you have been principal. Though you have been warned many times in the past due to numerous complaints, you did not heed our warnings. This was the last straw, especially when it pertains to something as important as giving a voice to those who have suffered a loss of this magnitude. Our decision is final."

"But...But..." Mrs. Randall stammered, looking absolutely flabbergasted. Her face then contorted in rage again. "FINE!! If you want the school to descend into chaos, be my guest!

Students will be running the school before you know it! Good-bye and goodnight!" She stormed out of the room.

After a brief pause, the viewing gallery exploded into cheers again, and I finally felt happy again. As I thanked every one of the board members, I couldn't help but start and formulate what our group was going to do to rebuild our support base and what we'll do for a kickstarter.

When I got back to the car, I was greeted by my fan base. As I got pats on the back and other accolades, I walked up to my family, and we all had a victory chat.

"When did this go from a simple meeting with Bruce Horner to a full-blown trial with the entire school board?" I asked incredulously.

"Well, Bruce wanted to hear Mrs. Randall's side of the story as well as yours, so he felt it was a good idea to hold a full hearing, especially after what had happened with the principal in the past." Jamie explained.

"Yeah, you should've seen the stupid restrictions she put on the clubs when *we* were in school." Anthony stated. "Me and the other members in the Pokémon card club were only allowed to meet in a room right beside woodshop, which meant there was insane noise the whole time, not to mention she forcibly disbanded the club, like, three times a year and we had to beg and plead for the club to be reinstated every time!"

"Really? Jeez, and I thought that Jeff's story of the robotics club was bad. Wow."

"I think the most 'wow-worthy' thing about tonight is the speech you gave!" Theresa exclaimed, giving me a massive hug. "You didn't even come to the meeting with a speech like that in front of you! Where did it come from?"

"I guess...they were just words that have been in my head since I found out about my group's refusal. I just needed a place to say them, and you guys gave me one."

"Well, if you have more of those in the future, then I think you'll get your point across no problem!" Marcus said.

As we piled back into the cars and headed home, I felt that I had just won my first victory in what was to be a long fight. When we arrived back in La Jolla, I steeled myself for what was to come next.

***

Our next day at school was one of insanity. When the school found out about the reshuffling of the staff because of my complaints, my status grew even higher and the amount of people joining and rejoining my group astounded me. The further news headline that Mrs. Randall had hacked the group's page and tried to ruin us also bolstered our new status. By the end of the day, I had over three thousand people in our group at school, and over nine thousand followers had come back onto our Facebook page, which had been restored.

This meant that we no longer could hold our meetings at the school as planned. After a week of planning and organizing, we decided to hold the first one down at Ocean Beach, due to the fact that most of the surf club was a part of my group. This was delayed by a week, however, due to the saddest part of my life: the funerals of my friends and father.

The funerals took place in the same week, back-to-back. There was a mass-funeral for the students in the gym, officiated by the local Anglican priest. Father Jacob's niece had been killed in the shooting, and his hymns were said in an emotional voice. The whole time, though I tried to keep myself together but as the names of the lost kids were called out, I wept at Colby's name and choked up at Becky's. Throughout the ceremony, I kept cycling through the memories we had made together, few as they were, allowing me to remain vigilant. After Father

Jacob finished, I was asked to give a speech by the new principal.

Getting to the podium, I looked out on the crowd and said, "I don't know what to say to you all that hasn't been said already. But I do know one thing. I assure you today that, while I am crying now, I will not let my sadness and depression overcome me. I was raised to be strong and to never surrender! I will fight so that no one else will *ever* have to suffer like us! This is my calling, my future! This is *our* future, and our *children's* future! I am now a fighter! For peace! For justice! For all of us!"

A loud round of applause responded to my words, as the families of the dead all applauded my words. Colby's mom came running up to me as I left the stage and she hugged me strongly. "That was brilliant, Nick!"

"Thanks, Robyn." I told her, tears still streaming down my cheeks. "I meant it. I promise you, Colby will never be forgotten. His compassion for me gave me a place here in San Diego, and I will make sure that legacy is put to good use. He was the most remarkable teenager I have ever met, and his death will not be in vain."

This garnered another hug from Robyn, and I could hear her sobbing as we embraced. "Colly was a man that loved life and loved you. I'll make sure I say good-bye for you."

As another flood of tears came to my eyes, I wept a thank-you and returned to my seat. As I sat back down beside Theresa, she hugged me strongly, and I returned the gesture.

"Becky would be proud of your work. At least be happy about that." She whispered to me, her tears spilling onto my shoulders.

"I will." I replied, returning the gesture.

After the ceremony, the families carried their deceased to their respective gravesites. As the Millers and I buried Becky, I knelt beside the gravesite as she was lowered.

"I'll never forget you, Becks." I whispered, tears flowing down my cheeks and onto her casket. "I'll never let your loss be for naught. You, Colby and Dad will be my encouragement so I can do this. We'll always be friends, especially when we see each other in heaven. Good-bye, my sister."

As we laid down flowers, my heart hardened, and I knew that I would keep my promises. We left a while later for a celebration of life dinner that night, and we had a much better time there than we had had during the whole day. The happiness was short-lived though, as the next day was, if possible, even worse.

***

The next day was an event I had never wanted to be dealing with for many years: my dad's funeral. It was completely different compared to the students'. It was at the naval base with full military honours, including an honour guard, a Stars-and-Stripes draped casket, and a twenty-one-shot salute.

It was the first funeral of its kind I had ever attended, and I am glad I hadn't had to do so before. At the funeral, I was introduced fully to all the men and women my dad worked with in the Navy, some of them coming from across the world for the ceremony. All the while, they regaled me with tales of my dad and his great personality. As my dad was buried in the naval cemetery, I noticed that he was surrounded by personnel that died in World War Two and the Gulf war. Again, as the casket was lowered, I spoke to the occupant.

"Thank-you Dad." I sobbed, kneeling at the edge. "Thank-you for making me the resilient young woman I am today. Thank-you for the life you gave me and the experiences you put me through. I will never forget them, and I will never forget you. Your friend will be here for you, just as you were here for me. You will be my motivator to fight my fight, just like you always told me to. Good-bye, Dad. Your little Nicky will always remain strong."

After the actual ceremony, I was presented my dad's many medals, his official uniform and hat, and the flag that was draped on his casket, which was carefully folded in the traditional way.

"Honorary Private Nicole Miller," said Admiral Brown, the commander of the base, "remember, don't unfold the flag, and place it in a prominent spot."

"I know just the place, sir." I responded, saluting him. He gave me the regalia, and I took them with a heavy heart.

He then gave me a full salute, and said, "Robert Grant was one of my best friends, and we have been so for so long. We graduated together from West Point and we have been in contact with each other for years. This was the first time we had been able to work together since we were stationed in the Philippines, and regrettably it was far too brief a period for the two of us.

"I also knew your mother, Nicole, and I know she would be very proud to see her daughter standing so strong in the face of such adversity. Johanna Grant was just as resilient and stubborn as you are, and I hope you channel her spirit as well as your father's as you move forward in your life. Good luck with your campaign and go forward knowing you have the support of the navy completely behind you. Thank you for putting up with us for all these years."

"It was my pleasure, sir, believe me." I promised, saluting him again. I then set aside the regalia and hugged the admiral, taking him by surprise. He got over the shock quickly and embraced me as well. The only thing that broke us up was a photographer taking our picture, which I felt would make a great headline for the local paper.

Later that evening, I took the mementos home to the

Miller's house and made a memorial to my dad in the basement living room, right beside one we had made for Becky.
Standing before photos of both of them, I then took a deep
breath and readied myself mentally, knowing that I had
work to do.

{ **11** }

Because Brochures Didn't Feel Adequate

The day of my group's first meeting had arrived. When I got to the beach, I realized that the crowd was so big, I would never be able to be heard by everyone. To combat this, I went to the surf shop and asked Laura's dad if I could borrow his megaphone (he used it to call attention to people whose rentals were about to expire). He told me to go for it, so I did.

When I got back out onto the beach, I stood on one of the surf shop's picnic tables so I could be seen and blew the siren to get everyone's attention. With everyone staring at me with hungry eyes, I realized they were expecting me to give a speech, just like I had done at the school board and at the funerals. Taking a deep breath and gathering my thoughts, I began talking.

"Alright, everyone, now that we're all here, let's get down to cases." I called out through a megaphone. "We all have started this group as a means to avenge the deaths of our classmates, friends, and, for some of us, even family members. We are all here to begin fighting for tighter, stricter laws surrounding guns and to eventually amend the Second Amendment of the constitution and prevent further gun attacks. Our high school was the latest, and worst, victim of a series of gun attacks that have now killed thousands of Americans, many of them children and teenagers.

"We are here to give voices back to those who have been taken away from us by a deranged alumnus of our school, and to give a voice to those who are still traumatized by the incident. We are here to show the world that we will not sit still and let this event hurt us! We are here to show that we are willing to stand up and end these attacks! We are here to end gun violence and mass shootings!"

My last sentence was drowned out by a resounding cheer from the crowd. As this rang out, I couldn't help but feel like I had indeed started something big. As the cheers subsided, I continued.

"On that note, due to the size of the group now, I feel that we should only get together in person on special occasions. We have been granted permission to form this group at Lincoln High, so we will have events and fundraisers in and around the school, but meetings will be strictly online unless otherwise stated. I organized this meeting so we can all get a feeling of just how much support our mission has garnered. We are now the Lincoln High Liberators, and we will not back down until we accomplish our goals! Who's with me?"

As another resounding cheer came from the crowd, my

heart soared. To think, just four months ago, I was just another new kid at a massive, very unfamiliar school, and now I was leading the school in a campaign. It was like I had been taken by God and replaced by someone else; I felt unbeatable.

"So, now that we have established our methods, we need ideas for fundraising and getting our mission across to the rest of the school and soon the city." I finished, looking around at the crowd. "Anybody got any ideas?"

"Yeah!" A voice called out from the middle of the crowd. "Give up!"

After a few confusing seconds, during which my group looked around to see who had spoken, I asked, "I'm sorry?"

A throng of about thirty people then quickly came storming up to the picnic table, shoving aside the crowd as they went. When they got up to the table, a person leapt up beside me and wrenched the megaphone from my hands.

"My name is Harrison Longfellow, and my friends and I are here to tell you that you are fighting a losing, impossible battle here. The government will never listen to your pleas, and the leader you have here, she's only doing this so her old pals in the military can take over the country!"

A collective gasp went up through the crowd. Then boos went around, with many people crying out conspiracy. My temper was rising faster than the space shuttle, but I chose to keep my voice even.

"That is a complete lie, and these people are telling you that you know it." I said angrily. As I looked at Harrison's smug face, to say I was scowling would be an understatement. "What are you *doing* here?"

"You, *all* of you, are fools!" Harrison continued through the megaphone. "You are fools to think that the government will actually do anything to help you! If things haven't changed in the past, who's to say they will now?"

Laura suddenly hopped up beside me and yanked the megaphone back. "I'll take my dad's property back, *if* you don't mind." She sneered. Though she was normally a quiet girl, whose hairstyle was generally a ponytail for her dirty blonde hair and her green eyes were hidden behind wire-rimmed glasses, there was a fiery intensity around her now that scared me.

She then turned to the crowd and said, "For those who don't know me, my name is Laura Vanscoy, and my dad runs the surf shop behind me. To answer your question, *Mr. Longfellow* (she mockingly exaggerated the name), of why we're fighting this battle, here's our answer: we have to try, don't we?"

A rebellious cheer came in response. As the clamour calmed, Laura continued. "If we don't show that the shooting hasn't gotten to us, and that we're willing to fight to end this violence, then the shooter has already won, even in death! We have to show the world that we won't let the status quo go on. This has to stop!"

A chant began with me and Laura of 'This has to stop!', and soon the whole crowd was following our lead. I glanced over at Harrison, and he had gone from smug to looking like he was surrounded by a pack of starving wolves and had on a vest of raw steaks. As I signalled for the chanting to stop, I turned fully to the man.

"Well, it looks like you got your answer, Harrison." I said playfully. Taking the megaphone from Laura, I said, "Now you *and* your little posse of poo-pushers, LEAVE!"

The crowd booed and cheered at the same time as the smaller group left with their proverbial tails between their legs. After a few minutes, I continued.

"Now, where was I? Oh, yeah! Who has ideas for fund-raisers and activities?"

A hundred hands shot up at once, so I decided to try and sort through them first.

"Alright, those who are suggesting handing out brochures, put your hands down now. We don't need those anymore." I called out. As a large number put their ideas down, I looked out and still saw about sixty hands up. "Okay, those who are suggesting a bake sale, put your hands down."

As a further number of people (I estimated it was about half the remaining idea volunteers) put their hands down, I took note of what had been suggested. "Alright, what do the rest of you have?"

I picked out Sam, who was right at the front of the group (she had been pushed down into the sand by Harrison's group, so she looked a little steamed). "How about a game night? We can have people bring games to the school and we can have students pay to play. And it doesn't have to be just board games either! We can set up a series of game nights, where one is video games, one is RPG and strategy games, one is card games, and one is classic board games! Maybe even one being for games like Pokémon. Sound good?"

"That's genius!" I cried to my friend, putting the megaphone down. Stooping down to hug my friend and whisper a thank you in her ear, I saw a lot of people interested in what she had to say. I then pulled her up onto the table with me and Laura and I put my arm around her shoulder.

Smiling at my friend, I returned the megaphone to my mouth. "My friend here had a great idea. For those who are not aware of who she is, this is Samantha 'Sam' Isaac, and she was a part of the cast of the musical. Her idea is to hold a series of game nights, each with a different theme and genre of game in mind. She also suggested to have students bring their own games and pay to play others. I think we should start with that! And don't get me wrong! A bake sale is also a great idea, and I think it will do great right before Christmas."

As the crowd began buzzing with conversation and ideas, I felt that the meeting was over. "Alright, everyone! I think that just about does it for tonight. We have our ideas. We have our mantra. We have a goal. We even have a slogan! Now, let's get things done! See you at school!"

With one last cheer, the crowd dispersed, some heading for the last waves of the night, some for the surf shop, others headed for their cars. As Sam and I stepped down, we were greeted by a wave of our friends. As I restored order, I began delegating responsibilities to my faithful companions. I declared Sam vice-president and, because she was on every platform known to the internet, head of communications. I also Pablo named in charge of finances, as he was a math genius as well as a surfing mastermind. I named Frankie in charge of promotions and events, as he was a very creative guy. And last but not least, I named Laura official venue coordinator, as her family owned or knew the owners of some of the best venues in the city. With all of that, I felt our first meeting was a great success.

***

The last week before Christmas was a blast. As I developed strategies to get our point heard across the city of San Diego, my colleagues were busy creating and organizing fundraisers. There had been a Super Smash Bros. tournament a week after Thanksgiving, and its organizers, the computer science club, decided to give us a good part of the money to start us off. When I asked the president of the club why he did this, he said that the club had lost five members when the lighting and sound crew were shot in the incident and they wanted to get back at the shooter. I told him we would and invited the club to join up; they did.

On the last day before Christmas holidays, we Liberators put together a massive potluck/bake sale where we all brought something from home and sold it in the cafeteria to our classmates. Sam, being a Jewish girl from birth, made her own brisket, which was arguably the most delicious piece of meat I had tasted in years. Frankie, whose parents were both Italian of origin, brought something called polenta, which he described as being fried potato pasta. This particular recipe was fried in olive oil and seasoned with what Frankie declared an 'old family secret'. Whatever that was, it was delicious.

I decided to bring a dish my mom had learned from my grandma years before I was born, a pot of meatballs with a secret recipe for sweet-and-sour sauce. It was an instant hit, with many people clamouring for more. The buffet that we had created was enormous, and every teacher was proud to be eating food cooked up by students.

Now, I know what you're thinking. 'How did you get three thousand dishes into one buffet?' The answer is simple. Just because there were three thousand people at the first meeting doesn't mean they all went to Lincoln and they were all students! Only about five hundred of the people at the first meeting were students at Lincoln, and even after that Frankie and I coordinated the events so that only a certain amount of people contributed to it. Fortunately, most of the people involved outside of Lincoln also had events in their own schools and offices.

By the time the Christmas holidays came around we had successfully planned over twenty events, organized and performed three, and raised over eighteen hundred dollars. What our next task was going to be was deciding on how we would spend the money. My initial idea was to pay for advertising of our campaign and get posters and other material together, but so much money had been gathered that I decided we would instead use it to pay for a trip to Sacramento or to Washington to protest in front of our government buildings. The group was quite pleased with this idea, and so we all pitched in to buy the stationery and the advertising ourselves.

As the Liberators all split up for the holidays, I decided to take a break from campaigning and just have a relaxing vacation. My first night off from school was a much-needed dead night, with me having been extremely tasked, both from school and work on top of all of the campaigning. As I sat down in an armchair in my living room, I nodded off and had a nice little nap, but was abruptly awoken by a pillow in the face.

"Hey!" I shouted, standing up quickly. I raised my fists instinctively and looked around. As I glanced around, I saw Theresa stooped over nearby, hollering with laughter.

"Wakey, wakey!" Theresa breathed, the pillow sitting at her feet. "Just thought you'd be interested in what we're doing for Christmas."

"Ugh." I groaned, rubbing my eyes. "Couldn't it have waited until morning? I've been looking forward to a nap for a long time!"

"Well, you can nap while you're on the plane ride!" Theresa hinted, chuckling.

"Plane ride?" I asked, confused. "Where are we going? Aren't we staying here for Christmas?"

"Nope. We're going to mine and Jamie's hometown of Burlington, Vermont. We always head home for Christmas."

"We're...we're going to be in a snowy world for Christmas?" I stammered, feeling very much surprised.

"Yes, of course!" Theresa said, indicating for me to follow her upstairs. "Christmas in Cali sucks! Palm trees look horrible with tinsel! Vermont may be colder, but it is far more, well, Christmas-y."

"Well, this will be my first time ever seeing snow at Christmas." I admitted, feeling a little embarrassed. "I was born and raised in tropical locations, and the only time I have ever lived in a cold climate was when we were in Seattle for a few months. I'm excited to see what winter is really like!"

"Well, pack for two weeks, and you'll find out! We're going to be gone until the third of January!"

"Will do!" I declared, feeling excited for a second, then something hit me, and I stopped in my tracks.

"Wait a minute, I don't have *any* winter gear! What'll I do?"

"Not to worry, you can borrow Becky's old stuff." Theresa assured me, putting her hands on my shoulders. "It's packed away for this very trip and it'll fit you great! I'll give it to you in the morning!"

"Thanks!" I told her, and raced away to begin packing, once again getting excited to try new things.

{ **12** }

Cold Weather and Warm Company

<u>7th December 2007; 1526 hours</u>

"Here you go, Nicky!" Dad says as he hoists me up on his shoulders. As he approaches the tree, I reach over and set the star upon the top and Dad plugs it in. It's a fake tree Dad had ordered online and had delivered to the navy base in Guam, but it is still better than having to decorate a palm tree.

As Dad sets me down, I look over the tree with admiration. The tinsel sparkles silver as it reflected the light coming off of the rainbow of light strings wrapped around the tree. The ornaments are a mix of those Dad had inherited from my grandma and some I had made as arts-and-crafts projects. The star is a light-up beauty that had come with the tree. There are already some presents at the bottom, and I am eagerly awaiting the time to open them.

"Daddy, it looks boo-tiful!" I say, grinning through my missing front teeth.

"*Yes, it does, Nicky.*" *Dad replies, ruffling my hair. "Now, let's get the stockings up!"*

When that's done, Dad and I stand back in our tiny living room and admire our work. The tree is bright with colour, and the two red stockings are hung around the wood stove, each of them with our names written on them. I also notice that Dad had hung Christmas lights around the roofline outside, making the navy base feel a little more festive during this season. Dad then steers me to the table, and he gives me a snack. As I eat some carrot sticks, he says, "You know honey, there's one thing I haven't shown you yet."

"What's that, Daddy?" I ask, sitting atop a pillow so I can see over the table.

"A movie about a green guy who hates Christmas." Dad responds, pulling out a DVD he had gotten from the base rental store.

"Who could hate Christmas?" I ask, shocked.

"Well, let's find out!"

***

<u>19th December 2020; 0645 hours</u>

Early the next morning, we headed to San Diego's airport. I was a little groggy, but my drowsiness could not hamper my absolute elation of visiting a place on the Earth that was nowhere near a naval station. Allan and his girlfriend, Anthony and *his* girlfriend, Jamie, Theresa and I met up with the twins and their families at the airport. After distributing tickets, submitting our luggage, and going through security, we sat down in a lovely lounge that had a view of the tarmac. As I sat near the windows and watched the planes with Marcus' and Samuel's kids, I overheard the men talking about seeing their family again.

"Can't wait to see Danny." Samuel said, thumbing the lock on his carry-on. "Heard that he and Cassandra are now living together and are thinking of marrying!"

"Yeah, can't wait to hear the news. I'm just anxious to see Auntie Kelly and Uncle Parker again. Their farm is the best place to have Christmas dinner."

"Nah, Grandma Lizzy's acreage is better. That hill in her backyard? Best place for snowboard practice. Besides, her dining room and kitchen are bigger."

"True, true." Marcus agreed, nodding. As he looked over at me, he asked, "Hey, sis, you're a little quiet. Aren't you excited?"

"Um, well, a little bit." I shrugged, looking towards my brothers. "I'm just a little nervous about how they'll react to me. On top of that, I'm a little sleepy this morning."

"Don't worry." Marcus said, waving his hand at the idea. "People in Vermont are the nicest people you could ask for! Minnesotans have got nothing on them! Our family will be happy to meet you, especially after what happened."

"Thanks, brother, that helps." I said, smiling weakly. "So, where are we going?"

"We're visiting both sides of our family, who live in and around Burlington. Our aunt and uncle, who are on mom's side of the family, are hosting one dinner at their place on Christmas Eve. Our grandma, who is Dad's mom, is hosting the other one on Christmas Day. Our gifts have already been sent ahead to ensure they're there in time, which is why you were told to buy them early."

"Ah, okay!" I said, nodding. "Where will we be staying?"

"At Uncle James' house. It's essentially our version of the family mansion, and we each have rooms there."

"Huh, cool." I said. Then something came to mind and I frowned. "Why didn't I see these guys at Becky's funeral?"

"To ensure enough space for everyone, the only people allowed to be there were immediate family. As you were a part of the family at the time, you were allowed to be there. They still called and sent their condolences though."

"Ah, now that makes sense." I said, looking back towards the tarmac. While we waited to board our plane, I was curious about what we were going to be doing while in Vermont.

Twenty minutes later, we were in line for the plane when something else came to mind. "What about Moon, Jack and my fish? Who will look after them?"

"Not to worry, it's all been taken care of." Jamie told me, smiling. "Ben, our next-door neighbour, always takes very good care of them. They'll be well taken care of."

"Okay, just wanted to make sure." I said, hoisting my carry-on.

We got on to our flight to Los Angeles, which was a small plane on a short flight. Our itinerary stated that we would be landing at LAX then quickly transfer over to our flight to Burlington. As I sat down and got comfortable, I resumed my curiosity for what was on the way.

***

Nine hours later, we were landing amongst the snowy mountains of Vermont, which was the first time in my life I had seen the white stuff up close. When we got through security, we walked onto the terminal concourse and were greeted by a pair of relatives, a man and a woman.

"There's my little brother!" The man said, coming up and hugging Jamie. He looked very much like Jamie, albeit with strawberry blonde hair.

"James, I've asked you not to call me that in public." Jamie replied, smiling.

"Ah, you can't make me stop, Jay-Jay!" James said, holding his brother at arm's length. "How have you been holding up?"

"Well, things have been going...okay. However, with my new daughter stirring things up in SD, I think we've *all* been doing well."

The woman suddenly went through a series of gestures I recognized as ASL, and James translated. "Isabella is wondering where the little lady is. I would like to know as well."

As I stepped forward, I raised my hand. "The little lady's right here."

Isabella looked down on me with warm brown eyes, her brownish-blonde hair falling in a curtain behind her head. The looks on hers and James' faces as they gave me a once-over made me realize that, though they still needed to pass judgement on whether I would be accepted or not, they wouldn't be harsh on me as long as I showed the same. Isabella then turned to James and signed some more. I recognized a few of the signs but they were made so quickly I couldn't read them properly.

"Isabella wants to know what your name is." He said to me.

"The name is Nicole." I stated, feeling a little uncomfortable. "Pardon my rudeness, but is Isabella deaf?"

"Mute, actually." Jamie told me. "She was born with her vocal cords unable to fully form sounds, so she has to use ASL to talk. Don't worry though, she can still hear you. I can teach ASL to you if you want."

"Actually, I kind of already know the basics. I may have to ask for some help on some of the more complex phrases."

"We'll help." James assured me. "Not to worry."

As you probably can guess, I'm your new aunt. Isabella signed, smiling. She kept the signs simple and slow, and I could read her signals. Her first sentence to me was actually *you-guess-I'm-you-aunt*, but I can pretty much interpret it. *You are such a polite girl. I can't wait to get to know you.*

"Same to you, Isabella." I said, returning her smile.

You can call me Aunt Izzy if you want. Isabella signed, spelling out the nickname. *Isabella is a fancy name given to me by my bourgeois parents.*

"Okay, I'll remember that." I said, walking to the baggage carousel to pick up our luggage. After we did so, we followed James and Izzy outside.

As we walked out of the airport, the cold hit me like a ton of bricks. As I gasped from the sudden temperature change, I couldn't help but ask, "Why can't everyone in the family come to *California*? Not that I'm complaining, but I'm surprised you guys want to leave the sun and the surf for this coldness."

As everyone laughed hard, I realized I had broken the ice with James and Izzy (oh, sorry, bad pun.) As he calmed down, Anthony replied, "Everyone has asked the same question for years, but we all have gotten the same answer. As Mom and Dad grew up here, they feel that this is their time to escape the chaos of Cali. They love the cold, and trust me, when we head home in two weeks, you'll be missing this place very soon."

"If you say so." I shivered, very glad that Becky's old jacket was providing some warmth.

As we walked into the parking lot, I saw that we were headed to a pair of vehicles, a large Ford SUV and a Dodge van. After we packed up, we piled into the vehicles. I was in the van with Allan, Anthony, Theresa and Izzy, with the SUV holding the rest of my family. After conferring on our route, we began driving into the city along Airport Drive, which we then turned onto Kennedy Drive.

Looking out across the city, there were green spaces covered in frost and snow, frozen rivers and streams, and tree-lined streets everywhere. Though I felt that the city would look spectacular in summertime, with all the trees fully leaved and green everywhere, the city still looked beautiful and cozy. As we crossed over a freeway, I gazed out and saw a snowy golf course and a series of parks across the city.

As we made our way into a more commercial area, and turned north, I saw in the distance Lake Champlain, a wide expanse of snow and ice dotted with little huts. As I looked out, I saw the lights of cars going out onto the ice.

"What are they doing, driving onto the ice? Is it safe?" I asked, concerned and curious.

Don't worry, it's cold enough to drive a tank onto the ice. Izzy signed. *The ice is thick and strong enough by now.*

"What are they doing out on the lake, anyway?" I persisted, frowning now.

Ice fishing. Every winter, fisherman from across the state arrive in Burlington with their shelters and go fishing through the ice. All the lights and shacks you see out there? Those are all ice fishermen taking up the daily catch.

"Wow, I never thought that they did that." I said. As we continue our trek, a pair of weird-looking machines pass by us. "What were those?"

"You really are a warm-dweller, aren't you?" Theresa said, grinning. "Well, if that's the case, we have to throw you right into the entire Vermont winter culture! We have two weeks to turn you from a palm-tree person into a winter wanderer!"

"And for the record, those were snowmobiles." Anthony explained. "They're fun to ride on. We'll be taking you on a ride in the next few weeks. It's time to cure your virginity to the cold."

As we all laughed, we turned off of the main drag we were driving on and onto a street called Ledge Road. We then turned onto a long driveway that led up to a massive house. The house was red-roofed and had white siding. There were a bunch of cars spread out around the small garage, which we parked the van into.

After unpacking the van, we walked into the house, and were greeted by a cacophony of cheers. I was then grabbed by a bunch of hands and was pulled into a gigantic living room. There were five new people surrounding me, all of them looking very much like my siblings, with the exception of a few of them having brownish-blonde hair like Izzy.

"Welcome to the Green Mountain State, new cousin!" A girl cried out, her brown eyes advertising great happiness. Frizzy red hair bounced around behind her as she shook my hand vigorously. "My name is Melissa! This is Patrick, Alison, and the twins Colin and Colleen! Welcome to the Miller family!"

"Thank-you, Melissa." I replied, smiling. I looked around and saw that the house was decorated with several old-fashioned heirlooms and paintings. The furniture also looked very old but in incredible shape. The walls were painted in a royal blue with wooden panelling running along the bottom half. There was a huge wood fireplace along one wall set beneath an elaborately carved mantle. Across the room from the fireplace was a massive wooden staircase, which ran along a hallway. From the smell wafting down the hall, I guessed that the hallway led to the kitchen.

As the rest of my family came into the room, Allan was laughing. "There's our welcoming committee! How's it going, cousin?"

"Al Ol' Pal!" Melissa shouted, hugging each one of my siblings in turn. "Merry Christmas everyone!"

"Merry Christmas," Jamie said. "Melly."

"Uncle Jamie!" Melissa said, blushing. "Don't mention that name until Nicole can get to know us more!"

"Too late," I said, grinning, "Melly." This spawned laughter from the crowd as we walked in.

As pleasantries were exchanged, I noticed a Jack Russell Terrier sitting on the couch. As I approached, the dog growled at me.

"Now, now Chilly." Alison said, throwing her long, straight, red hair back behind her head as she sat down beside the dog. "Be nice. This is Nicole and she's your new cousin!"

I walked closer and began petting the dog. Though he growled initially and when I sat down, when I found the right spot, he immediately warmed up to me. In no time at all, he was licking my hands and really settling in on my lap. The rest of the family sat down along a massive sectional and a couple of chairs. After a more complete introduction, we were soon exchanging stories, which carried on over in the dining room. There, we were served a delicious meal of honey-maple ham and mixed vegetables, which made me feel so comfortable I was already yawning.

"Don't fall asleep yet!" Alison told me. "Us adults are playing a game right after this!"

"Okay." I yawned again, stretching. "What game?"

"Monopoly." Theresa informed me. "We always play with teams, except for one person. In our rules, the one that plays on their own is the person with the most presents under the tree."

"And according to my count this morning, that person is you, Allan!" Alison stated, pointing at my brother.

"Actually, Ali, I have an idea!" Jamie suggested. "As she just joined the family, why don't we let Nicole prove herself!"

"You're on, Jamie!" I said confidently. "This is my opportunity to prove myself to my new family. I just have three words to say to you guys. You're. Going. Down."

"Oooohhh!" The family cried out, smiling and taking on my challenge. Little did they know, along with most of the people on the navy bases, I was a master at Monopoly.

After the little ones were put to bed, the game began. I was given the choice of my piece, and I took the cat (naturally). As we were dealt the money, I noticed they used an extender pack for the cash to increase the cash available. Soon, we were in the thick of a three-way show-down between me, Jamie and Theresa, and James and Izzy.

As I garnered all four railways and the waterworks, they got a hold of some of the hotter-ticket properties. Soon, the other partnerships dropped out and bankrupted as the five of us fought almost tooth-and-nail for Boardwalk and Park Place. When I got my hands on Park Place, I realized that I was on the road to winning.

Suddenly, Jamie and Theresa began teaming up with their former foes and ganging up against me. I soon found myself having to pay up on double the properties, and it was costing me big time. It didn't deter me, though, as I miraculously managed to get Boardwalk and began to bankrupt my new aunt and uncle. Even their tag-teaming didn't help, as Jamie and Theresa had to worry about their own moves.

At the end, after more than five hours of playing, I finally got my relatives to concede defeat. This generated a lot of laughs and praise from my relatives, and we all went to bed happy and hearty. I realized that they had, tentatively at least, accepted me into the family, and I was feeling ecstatic about it.

Making my way upstairs, I discovered that I shared a room with Alison and Melissa and was sleeping on an inflatable mattress.

"Yeah, yeah, I know, it's not exactly fancy accommodations, but with so many people in the house, this is the best we can do." Melissa said, pulling on a bunny-patterned sleepshirt.

I smiled at my two cousins. "It's perfect."

13

So. Much. Food.

The next few days in Vermont were devoted to enjoying activities completely unfamiliar to me. The day after we arrived, we went skating on Lake Champlain, and though I had a hard time at first simply standing up, I treated it just like I had when Becky taught me how to surf and I soon was good enough to go around without a chair in front of me.

Meanwhile, some of the family had started a pick-me-up game of hockey. I kind of knew about the game, but not much. The way the Millers played, though, it was clear that this was a regular sport for them. As I watched them, other people from the city came in and joined, creating a giant game that had to be at least sixty players strong. Many of them were wearing jerseys that had a certain logo on them, and as I sat down for hot chocolate with Theresa, I asked what the logo was all about.

"Well, considering where *you're* from, I'm not surprised you don't know." She explained, sipping from her own cup.

"That logo is for a team in the hockey community that suffered a loss as tragic as yours."

"Oh, no." I said sadly. "What team's that?"

"The Humboldt Broncos. They were involved in a terrible crash between their team bus and a tractor-trailer a few years back. The T-bone killed half the team with the other half seriously injured. It devastated the city their team was from, which is a tight-knit, family-like community. The whole hockey community came together and donated money to the families of the victims and advocated for the advancement of stricter laws on semi-truck drivers; they succeeded."

"Where did this happen?" I inquired, frowning. "You'd think I would have heard about this on the internet."

"All depends on when and where you logged on to. You were on another continent when it happened, by the sounds of it, and it wasn't exactly headlining news across America. It happened in the Canadian province of Saskatchewan, so we only heard of the incident when we were here."

"Ah, I see." I stated, nodding. It was then I realized that the advocates from this tragedy were victorious in their mandate, and I thought that this would be a perfect place to build an example of success off of. This was another thing I felt I could work with, and I was glad I had asked about it, heart-wrenching as it was.

After the game of hockey, or shinny as it was called by my brothers and cousins, we went back to the house to warm up and have supper. During this meal, which was a delicious spread of homemade pizza and pasta, we discussed what we wanted to do the next day.

"Well, if we're going to initiate Nick here into the Miller Family, we *have* to take her for a ski trip. I'm sure we all packed our ski pants and proper equipment." Alison spoke up, grinning.

"Yeah! I'd love that!" I shouted, spraying pepperoni into the air. As everyone laughed and gave me a chance to clean up, I felt embarrassed. "What I mean is that I would love to learn to ski. When I was living in Seattle, my birth dad promised me that he would take me into the Rockies to ski or snowboard, but we never got the chance before we transferred out."

"Well, seeing as we have some days to spare until Christmas," James said thoughtfully, "why not?"

As we all cheered, we cleaned up the pizza and, this time, went our separate ways in the house. Us 'kids' went down to the basement, where Colin and Colleen had a game room. There was the biggest flatscreen TV I'd ever seen standing above nearly every game system you could think of, as well as a massive pool table, a fancy dart board, and even an air hockey table. There was also a massive bookshelf stacked with board games, including the Monopoly we had played the previous night. I was amazed at the money the Millers had, but it was in that room that I got my next big surprise.

"Alright, now that we're finally away from the parental units, I think I can say what's been on my mind." Colin huffed, his usual nice persona gone. He turned straight to me with an angry and pained look on his face. "What makes you think you can just barge in and replace my favourite cousin, huh? Do you think you can just waltz into our family and expect everyone to love you? Well, do you?"

"Colin!" His twin Colleen gasped, her hands over her mouth in shock. "What's wrong with you? I thought you liked Nicole!"

"Well, you thought wrong!" He shouted back, turning to her briefly before wheeling back on me with a snarl. "You may have proven yourself to be a smart girl like Becky by beating us at Monopoly! You may act like Becky! You may even try and *be* like Becky, but you will *never* replace her!" He then crossed his arms and turned away, storming off towards a beanbag chair.

As everyone looked at me in stunned silence to see how I would respond, I felt terrible. I knew I had to say something, but I wasn't sure what. The Nicole Miller speech-machine was jammed as my emotions ran high, but I decided I still had to try. I hung my head and walked over to the chair. When I saw Colin's face, I noticed he was quietly crying.

"Colin, listen." I said gently, kneeling down to look him in the eye. "I don't want to replace Becky. I never have, and I never will. I know what you're going through is hard, especially at Christmas. This is my first Christmas without my father, and it's hurting me badly. I myself am not expecting Jamie to replace my dad, which is why I'm not calling him 'Dad'. However, I know that if we get to know each other, we can make our way through this pain together, and we can honour the memory of Becky. Trust me, I want to preserve her legacy, not erase it or take it over."

Looking up, Colin still didn't seem to believe me. "How

can I be sure? Becky, Allan, Colleen and I were an unbreakable quad squad. When we got together, nothing could stop us from having the time of our lives. Now that that's gone, do you expect me to believe that you'll be filling that void?"

"No, I don't." I admitted, a tear streaking down my face. "Becky was my best friend, and the first girl I could call as such in my entire life. My father was the only family I ever knew, as I have no siblings, cousins, aunts, uncles, or anything. Heck, I never even knew my mom! She died giving birth to me, and I've always felt a void in my heart that would normally be filled by a mother figure. I'm not expecting my friend Sam to fill the void left behind by Becky, and I'm not expecting the Millers to fully fill the family void in my heart. But our broken hearts can be mended if we do this together, and through that those voids will begin to feel not so deep."

I looked up at the other Millers standing back and watching. Many of them had tears running down their faces as they listened. "I love you guys, and you all will make a great surrogate family, but the void in my heart for my father will forever remain there. That's why I'm campaigning in San Diego, so that no one will ever have to suffer like we have. Can you accept that, Colin?"

Colin looked deep into my eyes, and as I looked back into his browns, I could see he was warming up to me a little bit more. Sighing, he said, "Yes, I can. I'm sorry if I got mad, but my grief has been hard to get over these past few weeks. I didn't realize how much you'd gone through and that you were in a similar boat as we were. Can you forgive me?"

"Only if you let me choose the first game." I said, smiling as I nodded towards the giant flatscreen and game consoles beside the chair.

"Deal." Colin replied, standing up.

As we began a tournament of MarioKart, I learned that my twin cousins were the youngest of the group, and were both eighteen, like I would soon be. They both were very smart and were in their first year of university. Colin, who had recovered well after he won his first race, described himself as an artist and was going to an art school for both drama and writing. His twin was the more scientific of the two and she, like her cousin Samuel, was at university studying chemistry.

Alison was twenty-five and a nurse. She was currently working in a detox centre for drug addicts, distributing an experimental treatment that helped get her addicts off their fixes. When I asked her how she had gotten time off, she said that her hard work and overtime had gotten her three straight weeks off.

Melissa, the girl I initially labelled as the leader, was twenty-six and a recent doctoral graduate of archeology from Princeton University. She specialized in researching the evidence of Vikings arriving in areas like Massachusetts, which seriously interested me. She said that she was close to finding physical evidence of a Viking longship in Boston Harbour and was getting super excited for the summer.

Patrick, a thirty-two-year-old entrepreneur, ran a series of bakeries in the Lake Champlain area, and apparently had honed his talents and techniques in business while attending this special skills school in Colorado. I wasn't paying much attention to what he was saying by that point, because then I was starting a race and I was fighting to stay in the lead.

As we continued on through the games, which included a Super Smash Bros. tournament and a crokinole championship, I began to fit myself in the void left behind by my friend. While we never officially talked about Becky after the argument, she was still brought up once. That happened when, in the middle of a game of Cards Against Humanity, I was accidentally called Becky by Melissa. Though this silenced us for a quick second, Melissa apologized, and we resumed our fun.

By the time we felt we needed to get some sleep, I felt like I had been put into a whole new world. Though I missed my dad dearly and felt a little bit of longing for the surf and sun of SD, I was already loving my time in Vermont.

***

A few days later, after a rather memorable ski trip (in which, yes, I *did* wipeout on my snowboard *a lot*, thanks for asking), Christmas Eve had arrived. I was explained by Theresa about how the dinner system worked. We would be having supper with both sides of the family on Christmas Eve, incorporating everyone except Jamie's mother, who lived outside Burlington; we'd be visiting her on Christmas Day.

"Why doesn't she join us at Uncle Parker's?" I asked, frowning as the two of us played a game of chess.

"She's a little too old to travel beyond the house." Theresa told me, grinning as she took my queen (I suck at chess, but I like playing it).

"Then why does she live on an acreage?"

"It's her inheritance. Jamie's sister Jenna and her family do the jobs around the acreage."

"Man, how big *is* the family?" I asked, removing a knight from the board.

"Very." Theresa said, chuckling.

"Why don't you have any more family?" I asked.

"I come from a small family so there aren't many people alive here." Theresa said quietly.

"Oh, sorry." I stated.

"Don't worry about it. Becky compiled digital family trees of my family and the Millers that live in and around Burlington for these visits and was glad that she didn't have to make them any bigger."

"That sounds like Becky." I laughed.

"And this looks like a checkmate." Theresa replied smugly, tipping my king over.

Later that day, after preparing our share of food, including a salad and a yummy dessert of the pumpkin pie variety, we all drove out of town to a farm right beside the middle of nowhere. As we arrived at the house, we were greeted by even more family members. This time, however, I already knew their names; they were the maternal relatives Marcus and Samuel were talking about in the airport.

"You must be Nicole!" Uncle Parker shouted, his booming, Scottish-accented voice ringing throughout the house. He had graying brown hair, grayish green eyes behind wire-rimmed glasses, and a body that showed that he definitely grew up on a farm. Aunt Kelly was standing behind him, and looked a lot like Theresa, from the red hair right down to the athletic figure. "Welcome to the MacGregor house!"

"Thank you, Uncle Parker!" I told him, shaking his hand.

As I stepped inside, I looked around and saw that it looked more like a hunter's lodge than the houses I had seen so far. There were heads of deer, moose, and wolves decorating the walls and a massive bearskin rug right in front of the living room's fireplace. That fireplace had an intricately carved stone mantelpiece and pillars and was surrounded by tall bookcases.

The living room, which was adjacent to the dining room, was directly to our right. Immediately in front of us at the door was a stairwell leading upstairs, and at the end of the hall was a doorway leading to the kitchen. Theresa and Kelly quickly broke away and went down to the kitchen, where I smelled turkey and gravy being cooked.

As we sat down on the couches and chairs spread pell-mell around the large living room, I was amazed again at the extent of my family. As we talked, I learned that Theresa came from a small, tight-knit rural family. Theresa only had Kelly as a sibling, but the two of them were best friends. Their parents had sadly passed away before I could have met them, but they left the massive house to them and had helped the both of them get into lucrative careers.

After a few more exchanges, most of which were so my family could get a sense of who I was, we were called into the dining room for dinner. We adults sat down at the main table, and the youngsters, which were Marcus', Samuel's, and Patrick's kids, sat down at the kiddie table in the kitchen. After Marcus said Grace, we began to settle down and eat. The main table, which apparently was an enormous oak creation created by Theresa's grandfather sixty years ago, was laden with dish after dish of food. Looking across the table, I had no idea how on Earth I was going to eat a portion of everything.

As we passed the dishes around, I loaded up with turkey, veggies, potatoes, gravy, dressing, and a bun. I decided to pass on a few things, like cranberry sauce, an unfamiliar dressing that smelled like pork, and the Caesar salad. Now, I know what you're thinking. *'That's a little rude, ignoring food like that!'* The thing is, though, I don't like Caesar dressing and cranberry sauce so those were reasonably ignored. As for the pork dressing, it didn't look very appetizing, so I decided to pass it by. Sue me.

Just as I was thinking this, Allan looked at me and frowned. "You're not liking Mom and Auntie Kelly's food?"

Blushing deeply and feeling terribly embarrassed, I looked at my brother and said, "Well, the thing is, I have never liked the taste of Caesar dressing, so the salad is off my list. As for -"

"He's teasing you, sister." Marcus said, rolling his eyes. "We understand that you'll never like everything. No need to explain yourself."

"Oh." I said simply, frowning right back at Allan.

"Just give the pork stuffing a try though." Allan suggested. "It's tasty."

"Alright."

As we began eating, everything was so good, including the pork stuffing, it made my taste buds forget every single Christmas dinner I had on the bases (or what you could *call* Christmas dinner there). I wolfed the food down so quickly, I was ready for seconds faster than what I thought was possible. After I began eating the seconds, Anthony burst into laughter.

"Hungry, are we, Nick?" He chuckled, wiping his chin with his napkin. "Man, I haven't seen *anyone* eat Mom and Kelly's food so *fast*! Are you at least *tasting* it?"

"Heck, yes." I said, finally coming up for air. "And it's the best tasting holiday chow I've ever eaten! This blows *EVERY* meal I ever had on the bases out of the water. You guys are *great*!"

As the family laughed hard, we resumed the eating, but as people finished, babble began to break out. As I decided to leave room for dessert, I set my now empty plate aside. I then struck up a conversation with the newest entry to my list of new relatives: Danny.

"The full name's Daniel." He said, twirling his fork around. "I'm seventeen and am going to high school."

"High school?" I asked. "When Marcus and Samuel mentioned you to me before, they said you had a girlfriend, had moved in with her, and were thinking of marrying her!"

"What?" He yelled, suddenly angry. "If that's the case, don't you dare believe them!"

"Marky! Sammy!" I called out. "What's this nonsense about Danny you were saying back in SD?"

"Uh-oh, she wasn't supposed to mention that." I heard Marcus mumble.

"Marky, I told you I was *dating* Cassandra and we were *thinking* of doing those things in the *FUTURE!* Not now!"

"Oh..." Marcus looked extremely embarrassed.

"Anyway." I said, rolling my eyes. "You got an idea on what you'll be studying after graduating?"

"Thinking of going into becoming either a math teacher or an accountant. I love math and stats so I would love to spend my life working with it."

"Wish I could say the same." I admitted, shrugging. "Still trying to find my place in the world."

"Are you kidding?" Danny stated, his eyebrows high. "From what I've heard from my cousins, you've been a little busy back in San Diego!"

"Yeah, well, I guess that's true." I replied, tilting my head.

"You *guess*?" Anthony yelled. "Sis, I have been telling this part of the family everything you've been up to since the shooting, and they have been *very* interested in meeting you so they can hear about your work better."

Actually, we all have been wanting to find out who you are. Aunt Izzy signed, putting her own fork down. It was then that I noticed that everyone had gone quiet and was expecting me to say something. As I looked around, I sighed and put down my cutlery.

"Alright, let me tell you guys a little story." I said.

14

My Message Is Spread Further

As I told my extended family about my story, what had happened to Becky and me during the musical and the subsequent rise of my advocates, it finally hit me about what I had accomplished. Though I didn't show it, I was astounded. I finally finished off at the group's last meeting, in which we were discussing our first march towards the capital of California.

Marching to Sacramento, are you? Izzy asked, looking very much interested.

"Well, yes." I said, nodding.

I have some advice for you about that that will *help.* Izzy grinned.

"Really?" I asked, now confused. "With all due respect, what do *you* know about protest marches?"

Putting his hand over his wife's, James smiled and said, "Your aunt actually has a bit of a rebellious streak herself.

When she was in college, she went on a hunger strike and led a protest rally to fight for the rights of handicapped students at her school. Though Helen Keller had fought for these in her time, some universities were restrictive on which degrees those who were handicapped could pursue. The college in question, which will remain anonymous, refused to admit her to Business Admin solely on her muteness, and she stood in front of the campus for three weeks, striving for her right to an education."

"Wow!" I cried, surprised. "Were you successful?"

You bet I was. Izzy signed with vigor, a victorious smile on her face. *During the weeks I was protesting, my parents brought together a legal team and we led a march of deaf, blind, and mute citizens that had been rejected like me. When we arrived at the courthouse, we had a group over a thousand strong and got the police's support. After another week, our trial was successful, and I was admitted into the Faculty of Business and Economics for the fall semester. Four years later, I graduated, and in my time, I had gotten computers and other devices installed at the school that assist in helping the handicapped succeed. Today, a scholarship to that school's Business Admin faculty is named in my honour.*

Feeling absolutely inspired, I said, "Holy crud. That is incredible. Now I feel like I *really* need to do well in my protest."

Meet up with me after we clean up here. I'll give you some pointers.

During said clean up, I was interviewed about my protest efforts. As I described my latest efforts, I was elbow deep in soapy water, wiping off dishes. I had told my family of our fundraisers and getting our affairs in order to perform the march.

"Well, I can definitely say that we'll be keeping up your fight on this side of the country." Melissa promised me. "With mom's knowledge and fighter persona, we'll make sure you guys have a branch on the East Coast and will be striving to get you a protest on Capitol Hill."

"Really?" I asked, turning towards my cousin. "Man, looks like I joined the right family!"

You sure did. Izzy signed, walking into the kitchen. *Becky was a valued member of our family, and the Millers do not let family members go down without a fight. We will not let Becky's death go unavenged.*

"Ah man, you guys ROCK!" I yelled happily, jumping up and hugging my aunt and cousin. They were clearly caught off guard, but they smiled deeply as I did.

The rest of the night went by with us playing card games and with me learning more about my family. Izzy was an investment banker at the local branch and James was a conservation officer with the Vermont Fish and Game Department. They had gotten two weeks off each for Christmas, though James was still on call just in case of an emergency. As for Parker and Kelly, they were both realtors in the area and ran their own office of the Vermont Real Estate Company.

I have to admit, by this point, I was getting overwhelmed by the amount of family information I was receiving. When I pointed this out to Theresa, she reminded me of the family trees Becky had created, and she also told me there were details on it that would help me. When we finally went back to James' manor, I was full of food and family facts. I felt like both my stomach *and* my head were going to explode. What I didn't realize at the time was that that night's conversation would become invaluable for me in the coming future.

***

We were woken up on Christmas morning in a most remarkable fashion: a loud air horn blaring from the living room. While Alison and Melissa were only slightly roused, I shot out of my bed in a shock, yelling incoherently.

"Whoa, whoa, whoa, Nicole!" Alison called out, while Melissa burst into laughter. "Calm down! It's just Mom calling us down for breakfast and presents!"

Clutching my heart, I said, "And she couldn't have had someone just *call* us down *normally* WHY?"

"Because that would be too boring for Christmas!" Melissa giggled, breathing hard. "And there's the fact that there are people sleeping on three different floors here that make verbally waking people pretty useless."

"Then why hasn't she woken us up like that before?"

"This is a sit-down breakfast for all of us instead of everyone coming down at different times and for small meals. This one is much bigger and yummier."

"Alright, in that case, let's go." I said, trying to relax, putting on my Pikachu slippers and smoothing my Frozen sweatpants and t-shirt. "Sorry, but those horns usually meant imminent danger on the bases. There's a reason I don't use an alarm clock."

"I'll remember to tell Mom that." Alison said, giggling.

As we made our way downstairs, I saw Allan laughing too, and I felt even worse.

"Thought I heard someone yelling upstairs." He chuckled. "Sorry, sis. Should have warned you of the, um, *unusual* way Izzy wakes us up on big breakfasts."

"Yeah, would have helped a tad." I said shakily.

As we sat down in the living room, I could smell something suspiciously like cinnamon coming from the kitchen, but Izzy refused to let us in there until the presents were opened.

Every new member gets to open first! Izzy signed, grinning as she handed me a small package. *This is from James and I and is our own welcoming gift.*

After pulling off the fancy golden ribbon and silver wrapping paper, I saw that it was a velvet box about four inches cubed. Opening the hinged lid, I saw it was a beautiful necklace, a gold chain with three gold letters in cursive at the front: B, N, and M. I looked up at my new relatives with absolute shock. My Dad had never gotten enough money to buy me gifts like this, so my jewellery collection was numbered in the zeroes.

"I...I...I don't believe it!" I told them, my mouth and my eyes completely wide. "*This* is a *welcoming* present?"

Yes. Izzy signed, her face a look of warmth. *This necklace is a custom creation that we feel is a way for you to go forward as well as remember the past. The charms are the first initials of yours and Becky's first names, as well as the first letter of Miller.*

With tears streaming down my face, I reached over and

hugged Izzy and James, mouthing 'thank-you' to the both of them.

"Alright, the first present has been opened." James declared, his eyes just as watery as mine. "Now, it's time to get on to the rest of the presents."

Those presents were just as interesting as the first, and ranged from a massive telescope for Patrick, who was an astronomy hobbyist, to a new set of pots for Izzy, to a huge set of fantasy novels for me. I got them from Marcus, and they were all by the same author. I was thrilled, as reading was one of my favourite hobbies. In all, over a hundred gifts were opened, and Chilly was having fun of his own as he jumped and leaped through the discarded paper pile.

After we sorted the presents, we walked into the kitchen and were welcomed by the smell of cinnamon I had identified earlier. The table was laden with platters of French toast, cinnamon buns, crescents, and juices. As we all sat down, we began passing the platters around. A babble of talk began, as we all started to compare our new gifts. As I chowed down on a crescent, Alison and I were talking about one of my new gifts, a lovely purple and blue wool sweater knitted by Izzy. I had decided to wear it to breakfast, and it was being admired by Alison. A little too much, by my standards. Before I knew it, Alison was begging for it, and I was trying to convince her that I wasn't willing to part with it so soon.

"No matter how many times you ask me, cousin, you are *not* getting my sweater!" I told her, shaking my head. "I like it and that's final!"

"*Pleeeeease!*" She pleaded, pouting.

"Alison Dawn!" James yelled exasperatedly. "You're going to make your new cousin regret she ever joined the Millers if you keep this up! Leave her alone!"

Everyone laughed as Alison blushed and returned to her now-cold cinnamon bun. I was so happy to have a family like this, I couldn't help but feel all warm and fuzzy both on the outside and the inside. As we finished eating and began tidying up, I was continuously smiling and feeling that, with all the new family members I had gained, the Liberators' numbers had just soared to levels I could not have imagined.

Later that day, we arrived at the Miller Farm, which was a short drive east of Burlington. After yet another series of brain-straining introductions, I finally got the feel for the family. James' and Jamie's mom, named Elizabeth, was a brilliant woman, and extremely happy to finally meet me. She told me she was born in Scotland and immigrated to Vermont during World War Two. She also informed she was a former police officer and was one of the first female cops in her county.

"It's been a fine life for me, grand-lass." She told me, her accent strong. "I'm impressed by ya! Heard you've been trying to rally people to a cause!"

"Well, something like that." I said, rubbing the back of my head.

"Well, welcome to the Miller clan!" Grandma Miller declared. "My old Beckster was the best grand-lass I could've ever asked for, but from what I've heard about you, you'll make sure she is never forgotten!"

This hit my heart deeply, and it occurred to me for the first time that the Millers expected me to live up to Becky's level of awesomeness. I wasn't sure I could do so, or even wanted to, but after the talk with Colin, I knew that they needed someone to take after her and help fill a hole in their hearts. I then settled on the mantra that I wasn't doing this mission just for myself anymore; I was doing it for the Millers, and everyone affected by the shooting as well.

After supper, I met my new aunt, Jenna, and her part of the family. There was her, her husband Adam, and their twin boys Jeremy and Jacob (what was it with twins in this family?) and their kids, all of them with green eyes and, with the exception of blonde-haired Adam, had flaming red hair. I was so happy to have Becky's family tree to help out this time, and I was even happier to meet my tiny little second-cousins. These two cuties, Brayden, and Thalia were still quite tiny but still a lot of fun to play with. My inner girly-girl was exploding as I became engaged in a tickle fight with them and with Marcus' and Samuel's kids.

When Jenna, whose full but non-preferred name I discovered was Jennifer, finally broke us up, we were told to darn our winter gear. When we were bundled up, we all marched up a large hill at the back of the acreage's yard. With the farm's lights providing artificial daylight for us, I recalled Marcus and Samuel talking about this place back at San Diego airport. As the younger kids immediately got down to business tobogganing, my siblings and older cousins either strapped on snowboards or donned skis. Meanwhile, I was a little unsure about what I was expected to be doing here.

"Um, as much as I love the view, what am I going to be doing? I'm too big for a toboggan, and I don't have skis, nor a snowboard." I pointed out, looking over at Jenna.

"Don't worry, Nick." She told me, walking over to a shed that was at the top of the hill. She came back with a large, air-filled inner tube and dropped it at my feet. "Here's your fun ride down."

"Are you *serious*?" I asked, shocked. I then watched as Anthony put another tube to his chest, ran to the edge of the hill, jumped, and flew down the slope. My heartrate sky-rocketed as I saw just how fast my sibling was going.

"Does that answer your question?" Jenna asked me, smirking. "Trust me, my niece, this will be the most thrilling ride you've *ever* taken."

Deciding to trust my family, I took the tube, said a little prayer, and jumped. As I flew down the slope, I was screaming the whole way. Going so much faster than I did while on skis, my heart went shooting into my throat. The only thing going through my brain was *'weeeeeeeeeeeee!'* I just couldn't believe what I was doing, but it was so much fun! When I finally reached the bottom, it was like I had just ridden a roller coaster, and I was so eager to try it again. But just as I stood up off my tube, I heard a sound that I had hoped I would never hear again: a gunshot.

{ **15** }

Why Must History Repeat Itself?

<u>27th May 2019; 1147 hours</u>

"Good shot, Nicky!" Dad compliments. I had just hit a bullseye with a new bow-and-arrow Dad had gotten me, and I was starting to get very good at it. As I pull back my next arrow, a gunshot rings out and my already-shot arrow is blown to shreds. I jump high in fear and clutch my heart as I pick my bow back up. Looking ahead, I saw what happened.

"Hey!" I complain, looking at the bullseye and pointing. "My arrow!"

"Who did that?" Dad calls out, looking around in anger.

"Sorry, sorry!" A voice calls out behind us. When I wheel around, I see a man with black hair and eyes like sapphires. His epaulettes showed that he is a navy SEAL, and he has a sniper's rifle strapped to his back. When he comes into Dad's sight, he stands at attention and salutes, which Dad returns.

All It Takes Is One

After being given ease, the SEAL continues, "Sorry, I was aiming for another target, and the arrow must have stolen my focus."

Sighing, Dad replies, "It's fine. Just remember to be careful when you fire, especially from a distance. My daughter and I had the range, and if you're going to shoot from a distance, make sure you leave enough space between targets to avoid this in the future. Now, may I have your name?"

"Petty Officer Second Class Malcolm O'Farrell, sir." The man replies. It was then that I catch on to an Irish accent, and I kind of giggle quietly to myself.

"I'm Captain Robert Grant, and this is my daughter, Nicole. We just transferred here from Bahrain."

"Ah, I see." Malcolm replies. He eyes me with a look that creeps me out, big time. "Well, welcome to Seattle, Captain! And you too, Nicole! I think we're going to make very good friends."

***

As our family looked around for the source of the sound, another shot rang out, and another, and another. Soon, it sounded like a war reenactment was happening next door. When I pinpointed the sounds' origin, I found they had come from the west.

As my heart chilled and my panic mode almost set in, Jamie yelled out, "The Descartes! The Descartes are under fire! Grandmothers! Get the little ones inside and call the police! Rest of you, let's go!"

As Jenna and Theresa raced the younger kids into the house, the rest of us ran towards the neighbour's house. The cowardly side of me wasn't sure why I was running to a place where I just heard gunfire, especially after what I had just gone through, but the other side of me wasn't going to let another mass shooting take place so close to me.

"How do we know that the Descartes' aren't just shooting to scare off a bear or something?" I asked, remembering the guards doing that at the Seattle base.

"They don't own guns!" James said, running like a cheetah. "They're strictly non-violent, and hunt with bows and arrows only!"

As we rounded the Descartes' front drive and raced to the house, a gunshot fired by us. We all hit the deck, and after a few seconds, none of us sounded hurt. It was then that my fear evaporated, and I jumped to my feet and charged to the house. As I neared a deck, I saw a masked gunman with a rifle looking straight at me. There was a light on behind him, and it silhouetted his figure somewhat.

"FREEZE!" He shouted out and aimed right at me; I stopped in my tracks, the rest of my family following suit. "Well, well, well, look who it is. I don't know how our paths crossed again, Grant, but I do know one thing. You should not have come here. You, of all people, should know what happens when you meddle in other people's affairs."

"Malcolm." I said coldly, recognizing the Irish-accented voice. "Malcolm O'Farrell. Well, it's nice to see you're using your navy SEAL training so usefully. What rock did you have to crawl out from under to cause you to do this?"

"Be careful, navy brat." Malcolm sneered. "I heard your precious Daddy isn't here anymore to protect you."

My anger erupted at the mention of my father in such a mocking tone. "WHO SAYS I *NEED* PROTECTING?" I shouted, and I ran straight for my old enemy.

Though he let loose a shot, I was running too fast, and it glanced off the deck railing. I ran onto the deck, dodging another bullet as Malcolm's aim became erratic. I tackled the idiot to the ground and yanked the gun from him. I then started pounding on him, punching every single inch of him I could reach. Though I saw blood beginning to stream from his mouth and nose, I didn't stop until someone yanked me back. I struggled as I was pulled off of Malcolm, and I was clamouring to get back on him.

"Nicole, Nicole!" Theresa shouted. "NICOLE! That's enough! He's unarmed!"

I still broke free of her grip and went back down. Deciding Malcolm was bruised enough, I just sat back down and pinned him to the deck, so his arms were unmovable. The position I held them in was one I remembered from my self-defence training in the navy, and it really appeared to be hurting Malcolm. I then ripped his balaclava off his head, exposing his black hair and blue eyes to the world. As I held him, I growled deeply and looked into his now terrified eyes, feeling no remorse.

As the rest of my family came and joined me, we heard a commotion from inside, and another voice called out. "Hey, O'Farrell! What's going on out there? I thought I told you to keep quiet!"

"There's a second!" James called out. "This whelp's just the lookout!"

"Get inside and stop him!" I ordered, fighting to keep Malcolm down. "I've got the whelp!"

"Quit calling me that!" Malcom yelled, squirming to try and free himself as James, Adam and Jamie stormed into the house.

"I don't take orders from you, remember?" I reminded the jerk. "You gave up your rank months ago, as well as my respect."

"Ooh, there's a terrible loss!" Malcolm growled, trying to shake me off but I sat on the backs of his legs, holding him fast.

"Nicole, do you know this creep?" Jeremy asked, frowning. The rest of my family around me looked concerned as well.

As I steadied my breathing, I began to talk, but then hesitated. The memory was so harsh in my mind, I couldn't decide whether I should, or even *could*, bring it up again. After mulling it over for a second, I told them.

"Yeah, I know him, unfortunately." I sighed. "Little Gunner Boy here was once a navy SEAL stationed in Seattle when my dad and I were there. That was last year, when I was still a high school junior. One summer's day, as I was strolling across the base and hoping to go for a swim, this moron here grabbed me from behind and pulled me behind a building. He then proceeded to try and strip my swimsuit off of me. He told me not to scream, and not to tell anyone what he was doing unless I wanted a gun barrel in my mouth. I then punched him, fixed my swimsuit, and ran to the base office. As I was telling my dad and the rest of the officers about what had just happened, Marmalade here –."

"That was my call sign, you bitch!" Malcolm yelled out, trying to free himself again. "You don't get to use it!"

"I'll use it as much as I *want,* freak!" I shouted, pushing Malcolm down just a little harder, breaking his nose entirely in the process. "Anyway, Marmalade here came running into the office and demanded that what I was saying was not true. He tried to convince the officers that I was lying, but my dad knew I never lied about things like this, and he had Predator Petty Officer here court marshalled out of the navy SEALS on multiple offences. And it turned out not just from my incident either. I did a little digging with my Dad around the base, and it turned out several girls and women were victims as well. At our behest, they came forward and told the commanders about Malcolm's attacks on them. He was *supposed* to leave Seattle, but he didn't, so that was when my dad decided to head somewhere where we could live off-base and be safer. That was when we moved to San Diego."

Shocked silence and stunned looks pervaded after I finished. The only sounds were from a series of undistinguishable shouts from inside the house.

"Wow. You have got a *lot* of bravery, standing up to this low-life after what he put you through." Melissa said at last, her eyes wide.

"Anger more than bravery." I admitted. "Nobody mentions my dad in such a manner and gets away with it. Not after the shooting."

As I struggled to keep Malcolm under control, James and Jamie came out with his partner, who was a grumpy forty-something in dark clothes. He had a nasty welt above his left eye and looked like he had just gotten stampeded by horses.

"You were supposed to shoot anyone who came near, you pipsqueak!" He snarled to Malcolm. "Not to get subdued by a *girl!*"

"Oh, shut up, Greystone!" Malcolm snapped. "It's over with!"

"Shut up the both of you!" I yelled, ramming my elbow into Malcolm's back, getting a satisfactory grunt in return.

"How are the Descartes's?" Allan asked, looking shaken. "Is Bradley okay?"

When the fathers looked away, I knew that we had another disaster on our hands. My heart crashed, not believing that this had happened again. As the rest of the family wept and comforted each other, I decided that I should screw our planned march on Sacramento and go straight to Washington. Things were now *very* personal.

"Are there any still alive?" I asked, my heart still plummeting faster than my recent run down the hill.

"Just two out of the *twenty* that were in there. Bradley and his little cousin Susie escaped serious injury but were still hurt. Even baby Percy didn't survive."

"*NO!*" Melissa cried out, horrified. She then fell to her knees and cried. "No! Not Percy! He was only six months old! I just babysat him last week!"

As James leant over his daughter to soothe her, I knelt lower, trying to get more comfortable. In doing so, Malcolm grunted. "Watch how you're sitting, bitch! That hurts!"

"I told you, blockhead, I don't take orders from you!" I

growled, sitting on top of him with my feet on his hands. "I never have, and never will. If it hurts then that's a bonus for me!"

"Never have?" Jamie asked, looking curious. "What do you mean by that, Nick?"

As I told them the story again, we bound the two crooks with rope. The police arrived just as I finished the story, and I was glad they did. I didn't think I could be around Malcolm much longer without killing him. After the police officers left with the crooks and gave us a lift back to the acreage, we all gathered together to mourn. It was an end to Christmas that no one *ever* wants.

*****

The next day, after giving our statements and getting permission from the police, we went to Burlington's community centre. There, the whole city had come together to honour the fallen family. News crews and cameras were everywhere, telling the story of this horrific tragedy to the rest of America.

As I talked with the people of Burlington, I found out that this family had been a staple in the community for years, and their deaths were a serious blow to the tight-knit city.

"Diana Descartes was a volunteer extraordinaire." The mayor said, her face sullen and sodden with tears. "She always worked hard to make sure the entire community was happy, well-fed, and had a roof over their head. It is horrible to know that she was killed for a mere home invasion."

"No kidding." I said, my heart feeling like it had fallen down around my belly button. As I moved on, I picked up a conversation with another person.

"The school division is formulating how we can honour and remember this tragedy." The man said, twirling a Boston Red Sox hat in his hands.

"What about naming Burlington High's school gym after Xavier Descartes?" Alison suggested. She and I were walking around together to keep from crying. She then explained to me, "Xavier was a basketball superstar, and he's been at the University of North Carolina for the past four years. He almost graduated with a degree in journalism. He set more school records at Burlington High than anyone else in basketball."

"Well, Ms. Miller, we'll keep that in mind."

After Alison and I moved on, the mayor came up to a podium. "Citizens of Burlington, thank you for coming. Normally today, we would be celebrating the holidays with our winter festival. Children would be playing in the massive snow fort built by our resident sculptors or taking sleigh rides around our scenic city. Us adults would be enjoying an ice-sculpture competition, an ice-fishing competition, or our annual polar-bear swim.

"But today, we are standing here, mourning the loss of one of the foundational families of our communities. Diana Descartes was a staple in all of our lives. Today, she would have been cooking up the massive pancake breakfast right here for everyone, and tonight she would have judged the baking challenge put on by August First Bakery. Her husband Maxwell would have been working on judging and deciding the winner of the ice-fishing competition and then participating in the polar-bear swim, which he has won five times in the past eight years.

"The children and their grandparents would have been working around the town, helping out and participating in the various games around our town. But now, only two of the seven survive, both of them in a panicked state of mind.

"We all know the Descartes family. We all know the contributions they gave to our community. Let us all remember those as we try to recover from this horrific tragedy. Thank you for coming out today. I hope we can come together and get through this."

After a round of applause, us Millers left. Later that day, after trying to improve our mood by going skating, we realized quickly that the shooting had essentially ruined our vacation. We then decided to forgo the rest of our allotted time in Vermont and take the next flight home. Two days later, we were wheels up and headed back to San Diego with very heavy hearts. Our vacation had been cut short, but for me, things were just getting started.

{ **16** }

The Capitol Gets Hill-Jacked

<u>*13th July 2021; 0900 hours*</u>

I was standing on a stage, chanting into Sam's megaphone in front of a massive crowd that must have been six-thousand, seven-thousand strong. We were yelling at the Capitol Building to end the violence, but so far, they had not even come forth to greet us.

It had been seven months since the shooting in Vermont, and the reaction had been overwhelming. Bradley had immediately joined my cause after his recovery, as did the rest of my family in the Green Mountain State. In fact, by the looks of it, they had brought the entire state of Vermont with them to meet me as I had marched to Washington. The entire Miller family in California had driven with me and my group across the U.S., performing demonstrations in various cities like Phoenix, Albuquerque, Colorado Springs, Kansas City, Indianapolis, and Columbus just to name a few.

As I stood in front of the crowd, I remembered the variety of speeches I had given. A shudder ran through my spine when one in particular came to mind, and my voice faltered as the memory came forward. It wasn't the speech itself, but the aftermath of it that had really gotten me on edge. It happened in St. Louis, and the city was as divisive as the Mississippi River itself.

"I stand before you here today, symbolizing that your city is indeed a gateway!" I had declared. They had erected a podium for me beneath the Gateway Arch, and though I felt dwarfed by the monument, I made sure my words were large and strong. I was looking towards East St. Louis and its own massive monument, the gigantic water fountain. Just seeing it and having the Arch above me made me feel stronger. "This city and state have suffered hardship just as much as San Diego has, so I feel that we can work together to end this violence. It is time for change! This has to stop!"

As the mob in front of me took up the chant, I felt happy. I could do this with complete strangers just as much as I could with family and friends. However, a few hours later, as we were leaving the city, we heard on the radio that the mob that was chanting with us had been attacked by another mob shortly after I departed. These attackers were made up of gun-enthusiasts that were against my protest. There were no deaths, but a lot of injuries.

"That won't help our cause." Sam had said that night. The two of us were riding together in the Miller's RV, and we were both feeling concerned. "But neither will us going back. We have to continue."

Feeling like I had to agree, I nodded. Nevertheless, I had a feeling that that attack in St. Louis was an indication of what was to come, and it would come back to bite us later.

Coming back to my Capitol rant, let me catch you up. We had arrived in Washington just two days before, after launching our trip on the Fourth of July at San Diego's navy base. We had left with the blessings of the victims and the victims' families from the Lincoln High Shooting, and had created a convoy of buses and cars that just kept growing with every city and town we stopped in. By the time we had arrived in the nation's capital, the convoy was over two miles long, with buses draped with banners and flags stating our intentions.

We had camped out in a secluded trailer park outside of town, and when we had permission from police, we marched together down the streets of Washington to Capitol Hill and began making our presence known. We had even garnered the attention of the media, with news cameras and reporters looking on at our demonstration.

When I stepped back and let Sam take over the chanting, I jumped down and joined Mom at a quieter side of the crowd (I had started calling Theresa that at her insistence after Christmas. It felt better after what had happened. Jamie, though, was still regarded as such, as I wanted to remember my dad).

"Nice work." She complimented me, handing me a canteen of water. "You really have started something here."

"And this is just the start." I informed her. "I got word this morning that there are more groups coming in from Maine, Florida, and even Washington *State* to join us."

"Gun violence is everywhere." Mom told me. "It's up to us to change that."

"If we can." I said, trying to sound positive.

"Hey, cheer up." Mom said. "I also got some news of my own this morning. According to my attorney's office, you are in the process of getting a date in the Supreme Court!"

"What? How?" I asked, surprised.

"Did you really think you were the only person working up a storm this whole time?" Mom asked me, grinning slyly. "While you were gathering up this army, I filed a full lawsuit against the Department of Homeland Security and the Department of Justice for not properly implementing and enforcing gun laws across the country. It has been appealed twice and is now going to the Supreme Court. The date is being set as we speak."

"Why didn't you tell me about this?" I demanded, a little mad at my mom. "And why wasn't I involved?"

"I told the court you were still dealing with the trauma of the Vermont shooting, so I told them to leave you out of it. Also, I thought it would be a nice surprise when we got here. Besides, I didn't think it would get this far into the system, anyway!"

After considering this, I just hugged my mom as we watched the crowd grow and grow. I then told her I loved her as Pablo took over and began a rap rendition of the chant (Pablo was a rap artist simply as a hobby and was always looking for an excuse to display his talent).

***

A few days later, after having a series of interviews with the media, the president finally wanted to see me. By this time, the Liberators' ranks had swelled to well over twenty thousand people, making it the largest protest in Washington since Martin Luther King Junior. The government realized now that they could not ignore us any longer and they decided to hold an interview between myself and the president.

Sitting in the Oval Office, I could not believe that I had come this far. As secret service agents stood by me, I awaited the arrival of the newly sworn-in president. I had followed the 2020 election deeply and was careful of whom I recommended the Millers vote for. Fortunately, the winner of the race was one who was a deep advocate for change, including gun violence. Suddenly, just as I was looking closely at a spot on the back of my hand, a door opened, and the president stepped in. She was in her mid-fifties, but she brought many years of experience in the legal system.

After the cameras were set up, she beckoned me over to a couch in front of the massive fireplace. As we got comfortable, the president looked right into my eyes for a second, then indicated for the cameras to start filming. We were counted in and the interview began.

"So, you are the famous Nicole Miller." The president said. "You are quite a feisty and fierce young woman. I have followed your campaign from the very beginning, and I have to say it has been a huge rallying cry for those who want to see change in the gun laws of America. You have done very well in bringing the country together."

"Thank you, Mrs. President." I answered, feeling extremely nervous. "I believe that *something's* gotta give, and I don't know how much more people this country can lose before our governing bodies realize that."

"Well, I do hope we can create a compromise that favours all of us."

"I believe we can, Mrs. President." I replied, my confidence rising. "I am not trying to rid this country of guns entirely. What I am advocating for is the restriction on when, where, and why a person can carry a firearm. I believe that this will help instill better control of guns and begin to eliminate the threat of people just waltzing into random locations and opening fire."

"You bring up some very valid points, Miss Miller." The president stated, looking at me deeply. "And I know my party and I will do everything we can to ensure you and your, um, contingent are well taken care of and given ample security. This is a rally that is needed, and it is time to end this crisis once and for all."

That last line stunned me to the core. I was completely shocked at what I was hearing, and, though I didn't show it to the camera, my mental jaw dropped right to the floor. After bringing my mind together, I asked, "With all due respect, Mrs. President, are you sure that you're going to be able to *do* that? I mean, yeah, you made it a mandate of your election campaign to end this, but I didn't expect you to be so, well, *on board* with us."

"The government has undergone a serious change over the past campaign. While we still have a great deal of senators and representatives that are very much against your ideals, it is a wide consensus today that we need to put an end to mass shootings. With your mother's case in the Supreme Court and you being here in Washington with a delegation that outnumbers most rock festivals, I think it is safe to say that it can no longer be ignored. I have also begun to negotiate with Mexico an agreement to have tighter border security on both sides so that the illegal drug trade and the gun trade can be mitigated."

"Alright then." I said proudly, feeling even stronger. "If you believe that Congress and the Senate will begin to hear sense, then I'm with you to the end."

As the interview ended, I was escorted out of the White House. When I reached outside, there was a wall of people in front of me. Reporters swamped the front steps and began asking me a massive amount of questions. Luckily, the secret service escorted me through the mob to an awaiting car that would take me back to our campsite. After finally sitting down in the car, I took a deep breath and slumped into my seat.

"Man! I didn't think I would get this popular. You'd think, the way they're acting, that I was some sort of celebrity or something." I mumbled to myself.

"But you *are* a celebrity, Nicky." My guard said. He removed his shades briefly, revealing his familiar gray eyes.

"*Dixon?*" I cried, amazed. Dixon Green was an old friend of mine and my dad's from our time in Guam. He had been part of the security detail at the base, and the three of us had gotten to know each other quite nicely. That is, before Dad and I transferred out.

"It's actually *Agent* Dixon, now." He corrected me. "I decided to transfer to Washington when I was offered the opportunity to work in the secret service. Just, don't tell anyone you know who I am."

"Deal."

"I am *so* happy we can see each other, my old friend. Your father would be so proud of what you have accomplished here."

"Same to you, agent." I said, smiling. "And thanks.

"Anyway, with this crowd and buzz you've started here, you *are* a celebrity to millions of people. I have a feeling that, if they allowed it, half the country would be here and swamping the city. That would teach the government a thing or two."

"Wait, Dixon, that's IT!" I shouted. "That's what I need to do to ensure that the government sees the spread of this. Not only do I need to coordinate this massive march here, but I also need to have all the people that couldn't come here to march on their respective government buildings and protest in their respective communities. There are enough people in these communities to make a substantial difference, and it will spread virally across the nation so that nobody can ignore this. *Nobody* can deny our intentions. We will fight this coast *to* COAST!"

As I looked at Dixon again, his mouth was wide open. "That was brilliant, Nicky! With the president on your side and that plan, you'll be winning over the hearts of *hundreds* of millions of people and finally stop this!"

"I owe you big time, dude. Now, time to think this out."

When Dad Taught Me That 'Words Hurt', I Don't Think He Meant Like This

A week later, my rally had exploded in size even more (if that was even possible). I had contacted my friends in seven different state capitals and on various bases. Within days, they had begun their own marches on their respective capitol buildings and head offices. By the time we had been in Washington for ten days, our rally was in eight states, as well as Guam, American Samoa, D.C., and even Canada! Thanks to this, our group was now numbering around the three *million* mark in population worldwide. Dixon's idea to go nationwide had gone further than I ever could have expected, as military bases across the globe began to sympathize with us. Soon, people saw our protest as more of a revolution than anything else.

"This is bigger than I ever could have imagined." I said, completely taken away as I looked down at the map of our progress. Over ten cities, fifty towns, and twenty global bases were on board with us and were convincing the government to change. I had on capri jeans and a purple shirt that had once belonged to Becky. "What have I started?"

"You wanted change, and you've gotten it." Sam told me, shrugging. She was sitting beside me in a camp chair next to her tent, painting her nails. The two of us were sitting between three tents that housed the executives of the Liberators and were resting in front of our fire after a long day of protesting in front of the Supreme Court building (mom's case had finally begun and was being made a top priority for the court). She had on cut-off denim shorts and a Hello Kitty patterned tank top. "Shoulda known you'd be getting this kind of attention."

"I suppose." I admitted, shrugging myself. "Well, tomorrow is my big presentation in front of Congress. Do you think those old codgers will listen to us?"

"I don't think they have much of a choice. The military is backing us up thanks to your dad's old friends from the bases, you've rallied hundreds of other protest groups to your cause, swelling your ranks to a size unseen in this country since the Civil War, and you've got a mom whose court case has reached the highest level in the land! You've reached places most others could only dream of achieving, and you're still going!

"The government, I think, will finally have no choice but to accept the fact that the Second Amendment is not one to have during peace times. Your idea in the first place is one to rally behind, and millions of people are now doing just that to show the government that, if they don't do *something* to fix this, they're going to have another civil war on their hands, just as you predicted."

"Man, and I thought *I* was the great orator of this group." I joked, impressed by my friend's impromptu speech. When I sat down in my own camp chair, I asked, "Hey, have you heard from San Diego lately? Wonder what's going on back there."

"Well, Laura's holding her own rallies at the surf shop with her dad, creating a massive following for you there. From what I heard from her, her dad is giving you all the time off you want to do this. He's hired a few people from the rallies to work your position while you're gone, and he said that business is booming so much, he may be able to retire in a little while and leave the shop to Travis."

I let out a little squeak at the mention of Travis, who was Laura's big brother. He had been encouraged to join our rallies in San Diego after we got back from Burlington, and he had taken on a strong duty of garnering support from the colleges and universities around the city. He was also a friend of Allan's, and his track-athlete physique, kindness to animals and strong mind had gotten my attention. Though I was still determined to remain loyal to Colby, I couldn't help but feel flustered every time Travis was around.

When she heard the squeak, Sam looked up from her nails and giggled. "Got something you wanna share, my friend?"

"No!" I shouted a little too quickly. I then blushed and corrected quietly, "Yes."

Laughing more, Sam asked, "Do you like Travis? As in, *really* like him?"

"Um, well, uh, maybe." I peeped, my face heating up. "I dunno, I mean, I wanna keep mine and Colby's love alive, but when Travis came into the picture, I became conflicted."

"I'm sure Colby would want you to be happy, no matter what. I say, as long as you remember Colby's love, you should go for Travis. He's just a year older than you, and while he is in university, thanks to you graduating last month, so are you! You've gotten yourself into UCSD and are well on your way to becoming a great scholar! He really respects you, and with your celebrity status right now, I have a feeling he's going to be clamouring to be with you when we return to SD."

"I hope so." I said, feeling a little more hopeful for myself.

It was then that some kind of shouting came from the perimeter of the encampment. Stuff like that happened frequently, as people cheered and got honks from passing cars, but this yelling seemed different. It didn't stop quickly as was the norm, and it sounded more panicked than excited. As Sam and I glanced at each other, confused, I began to feel really uneasy about what was happening. A couple minutes later, Mom came bursting onto our site, breathing heavily and a look of panic on her face.

"Mom! What's wrong?" I demanded, leaping to my feet.

"Gun-enthusiasts are attacking the camp!" Mom shouted, bent over as she caught her breath. "They're looking for you!"

"Oh, no." I stated, my blood chilling again. Earlier in the day, our latest rally had included me belittling gun-enthusiasts a bit, but I felt I did so off-handed. I never meant it to be taken seriously! "Those guys have probably hit their boiling point. Are the police on their way?"

"FBI and D.C. police are sending their riot squads, but it might take a bit." Mom informed us.

"I have to go to them, then." I said, steeling myself for any punishment I would encounter.

"Are you *CRAZY?*" Sam shrieked, shooting to her feet herself. "They'll eat you alive!"

"Fair punishment for my stupid comments this afternoon." I pointed out. "I led these campers here, and it is my comments that brought the gunners here. I am the leader here, and it is my responsibility to lead them. I'm going."

And without any further ado, I took off running towards the sounds.

"Nick, wait!" I heard Sam scream, but I ignored her. Racing around the tents and trailers, the sounds just got louder and more violent. I was glad I wasn't hearing any gunshots, but I wasn't going to slow down for that. I passed cluster after cluster of campers, many of whom were curious as to what the shouts were.

"Nick! What's going on?" Anthony yelled as I passed him and Allan on their way from the woodpile.

All I could say was "Tell you later!" before I continued on running.

As I rounded the last corner, I came to a scene of absolute chaos. Tents were on fire, and there were men and women slicing and thrashing the RVs and remaining tents with knives and hammers. A few even had lighters and they set the downed tents on fire as they passed. Every one of them had guns strapped to their backs and in holsters on their belts. One guy in particular was standing on the back of a pick-up truck and calling out through a megaphone.

"Where is Nicole Miller?" He announced, raising a pistol into the air. "If you don't surrender her, we'll drop the steel and bring out the lead!"

People were scrambling to get away, but the intruders were holding the stragglers fast. I saw people who had come from all over North America now being held at knife point, all because I had said some mean words earlier. I shoved my fear aside and stood up tall.

"HEY!" I screamed. Almost simultaneously, every attacker stood up and stopped what they were doing.

Chuckling evilly, the leader looked down on me. "Well, well, well, about time you showed up, missy. I was beginning to think you were just as cowardly as you sounded on the tube earlier."

"Leave my friends alone." I demanded, my deathly calm voice seething with anger. "It's me you want."

"Very well." Truck-Guy said gruffly, signalling his posse to release my friends. As everyone fled to safer parts of the camp, I was left by myself.

"Alright, now that we have *that* settled," I said, my voice shaking with anger, "what is it you want with me?"

A shot rang out from Truck-Guy and my left arm exploded with pain. As I fell to my knees, gasping, I heard the pistol reload. I released my hand from my shoulder, and saw it coated in blood. My vision went fuzzy as I reeled from the sight, but when I heard the safety release from the pistol, I shook my head to clear it and looked up.

"You made us sound like fools, little lady." Truck-Guy growled, his twangy accent sounding scary in this situation. "And George McTavish is no fool! You have to be careful about what you say while on camera. What was it you said? Oh, right, it was that 'all gun-enthusiasts are drunken hillbillies that shoot for fun.' That is a mean stereotype, just as much as callin' a native an Indian. Take back those words, or I start aimin' better."

"Fine!" I shouted, trying but failing to get onto my feet. "I-I'm sorry for my comments. They were dumb. I take back what I said earlier. You're...you're right."

"Good to hear that. I'm here to say that it is our right to have guns, it has been for two-hundred and thirty years, and it will be forever. Give up on your quest!"

"I'm...not...trying...to end that right!" I stammered as I finally rose back up, my body shaking hard. "All I desire is to change it so that conflicts like this are stopped and mass shootings no longer happen."

"I don't care!" George shouted, taking aim once again. "You have no-"

"NO, I HAVE EVERY RIGHT!" I interrupted, my anger exploding as I focused on my opponent. "FIRST AMEND-MENT, FREEDOM OF SPEECH, REMEMBER? OR IS THE ONLY PART OF THE CONSTITUTION THAT MAT-TERS TO YOU THE SECOND AMENDMENT?"

Another shot rang out, hitting the ground between my

feet. I nearly lost my balance and fell over as I leapt back. "You have no idea-" George began, but I cut him off again.

"NO, *YOU* HAVE NO IDEA WHAT *YOU'RE* TALKING ABOUT!" I screamed, my face contorting in both fury and pain as my shoulder wreaked with suffering. "I LOST THE ONLY PARENT I'VE EVER KNOWN, MY FIRST EVER BOYFRIEND, MANY OF MY FRIENDS, AND FULL USE OF MY RIGHT ARM DUE TO AN ATTACK! THEN I SAW NEARLY AN ENTIRE FAMILY GET DECIMATED AT *CHRISTMAS TIME* DUE TO GUN-TOTING THIEVES. HOW MANY MASS-SHOOTINGS HAVE *YOU* BEEN A VICTIM OF OR SEEN FIRST-HAND?"

"Uh, um, well." George said, looking shocked at my reaction.

"I thought so." I snarled.

"Hey, girl, don't you talk to me like...OOF!" That last part was due to the random event of a police officer jumping up and tackling George out of the truck. As I looked around, I saw that I had distracted the attackers long enough for the police to apprehend the entire posse. I then fell back to my knees in relief and tried to steady my breathing. My tension released and I blacked out.

***

I woke up a few minutes later on a gurney with a paramedic looking down at me. I looked around and saw a much calmer scene than when I arrived. The attackers were being led away, and the campsite was being cleared of debris.

After a few minutes, an FBI agent came up to me and took in my statement.

I apparently was still bleeding hard from my graze, but it was in a bandage now and the pain was beginning to ease. After taking in my version of the events, the agent sighed and looked around the site. Several tents were either slashed, trampled, burnt to a crisp, or all of the above, and several RVs had been damaged. Though I was internally elated that no one was killed, the fact that there were several serious injuries made me feel really guilty.

"It wasn't your fault, you know." The agent said. "These punks were planning to do this regardless of what you said."

"Be that as it may, my words wound up hurting people, and I can't let this happen again."

"Well, I would think carefully of the words I'd be saying at Congress tomorrow, if I were you. They, and this attack combined, may prompt stronger action by the government or more aggressive attacks by other groups. You'll need to tread very carefully from now on."

"Thanks, officer, that kind of helps." I said, slumping to my butt as the paramedics began to look at my arm again. It was re-examined and my arm injury was found to only require a new gauze pad and some cleanser. As I watched other injured people from my camp head to hospital, I felt that my speech to Congress would make or break our efforts. It was time for round three.

{ **18** }

I Step Up

<u>23rd July 2021: 0930 hours</u>

As I stood up in front of the House of Representatives, my shoulder was throbbing, and I was feeling terribly drowsy (I hadn't slept at all the previous night). But that didn't stop me from trying to look strong and determined in front of the elected officials. This was the final tipping point for my efforts. If I failed to get the approval and support of these men and women, I might as well go back home to La Jolla and be done with it.

After the order was called, the speaker announced, "The house recognizes Nicole Miller, daughter of the late Rear Admiral Upper Half Robert Grant and leader of the Lincoln High School Liberators, the group that is demonstrating in our city. Ms. Miller, you have the floor."

Clearing my throat and calming my nerves, I began my speech. "Thank-you Mr. Speaker. Honourable Electorates of the United States of America, I stand before you all because our country is being threatened. And when I say threatened,

I mean from within. As you are probably aware of, last year, San Diego's Lincoln High School was the venue for the most devastating mass shooting by a single shooter this country has ever seen. That attack lost us forty innocent lives, including the aforementioned Robert Grant, one of the US Navy's most respected and beloved officers and my most loved father. He died trying to save my best friend, Rebecca 'Becky' Miller and my boyfriend Colby Anderson, but unfortunately, he was unsuccessful."

"I myself was injured in this attack as I tried to subdue the shooter, Carl Fillmore. I was raised on the belief that fear comes after action, and despite my fear of guns, I wasn't going to let this thug ruin our school's musical. Sadly, I..." I stopped there as I choked up, the memory coming flooding back to my mind. Pulling myself together, I continued. "I wasn't able to stop the shooter, and he threw two grenades into the crowd, causing more deaths and more injuries. After I recovered from my injuries, I decided that things needed to change.

"My father had mentioned to me years ago that the Second Amendment was creating a serious issue in our home country, with the mass shootings across nearly every state and happening to nearly every class, race, political belief and income level between our borders. When the man that described that to me was killed by the very thing he was a hater of, I took it upon myself to create a protest group at my school so that those who were affected by the attack would be able to channel their emotions into something useful.

"As we connected with others in San Diego, our numbers

grew into the thousands. When the police released their report on the incident, they found that Fillmore was a former, failed student of Lincoln High School that had decided to get revenge on the school. He felt that it wasn't his skills that had failed him, but the school system itself, so he took his rage out on the school, starting with the drama teacher that encouraged him that he would succeed. When those facts were released, we found support from other groups and advocates from across California.

"Then, when Burlington, Vermont suffered its own mass shooting this past Christmas, which, luck would have it, happened right next door to my new family's acreage, I gained help from the other side of the country. As the months went by, we used social media and email to connect with more and more people, and we hosted enough fundraisers to save up enough money to create this march. By the time we left San Diego, we had about eight hundred and fifty thousand supporters. When we arrived in Washington, that number had expanded to well-over three million people on Facebook alone. And that didn't include the seven thousand we have camping with us."

"Our tour of America while marching here got us support in several states, and that support is now creating their own protests in their own state capitals. These past couple weeks in Washington, we have shown our stance, and our will. I have had multiple interviews with the media, which has further cemented our status.

"Last night, however, we ran into another hurdle. Despite having the president's approval and her backing of our cause, as well as the promise of security, a gang of gun-enthusiasts attacked our camp, injuring several of our supporters and the security detail that surrounded that gate. That is how far this crisis has become: attacks in our own nation's capital on peaceful protestors! And now, I hear my supporters across the country are facing equally stiff opposition in their protests! These are creating stand-offs where there are two warring parties protesting against each other in front of the government. Is that how we want our country to look? Because it looks to me like we are close to another Civil War erupting if this is not stopped. The first Civil War was fought based mainly on a right that many felt was their own, and nobody could take it away. If we don't do something soon, we will be in a similar situation."

Taking a deep breath, I continued. "As I sat in the camp nursing my wounds last night, as I saw what I had created, I realized that it was up to me alone to ensure the safety and security of my group as well as continuing our campaign. On that, here is my pledge: We, that is, the Lincoln High School Liberators, are not here to demand the Second Amendment get rejected. We are here to advocate changes to the amendment to the point that it will become more difficult for a person to purchase and access firearms. We also want to ensure that it is illegal for those who own guns to simply carry them around on their person unless they are hunting, or the guns are a part of their job *and* they are on duty.

"We have discussed and compared our manifesto with friends we have gained from Canada and they have given us a plethora of references to use as comparisons. They believe that it is going to be difficult to convince everyone here to follow our ideas, but they have given us the idea that anything is possible, so, let us start. Thank-you."

After a generous amount of applause, I finished with, "I will now open the floor to questions."

When one representative stood up, the speaker recognized him as the representative of Alaska. "Thank-you for that impassioned speech, Ms. Miller. While I have been elected by the citizens of Alaska to represent their opinions and ideas and bring them to Washington, I cannot help but agree with what you just stated. Too often I have walked down the streets of my hometown of Anchorage and seen hundreds of people with guns on their person for nothing more than a deluded desire for self-defence.

"This doesn't seem to fit the security of the city, as it has one of the lowest crime rates in the country. I feel that, at any time, one of those gun holsters will be empty and lives will be in limbo. I motion that we make changes to this amendment so that, at the very least, people cannot carry guns everywhere they go."

A much more mixed response echoed around the room this time, and it sent a chill down my spine.

"Order! Representatives, we shall have order!" The speaker called. "I now recognize the representative for Arkansas' 2nd congressional district."

Standing up, the representative looked right at me. His chinless face and beady eyes didn't seem intimidating, but I've learned the hard way not to underestimate people. "Ms. Miller. I do see the position of your stance, and I can assure you that you have the entire state of Arkansas' sympathy for your loss. However, I hope you understand that what you are proposing is not going to create the same kind of sympathy in a vast number of my constituents. Many of them feel that the Second Amendment is fundamental and is a requirement in their lifestyles."

Sitting down, the representative and his colleagues seemed to expect a response. Taking another deep breath, I replied. "I completely understand that some people are not on board with my group's stance. I am not looking for unanimity in this proposal. What I *am* looking for is for our government to finally recognize that the amendment needs to be changed. I am positive that we can make compromises that will benefit the majority of the country and will make our streets and public gatherings safer. It is time we did away with the generalization that the amendment brings and create stronger and more concrete laws to direct gun use.

"It is the belief of the Liberators that the amendment is just too vague for this day and age and was created during a time when settlers were under constant threat from other settlers, dangerous wildlife, Native Americans, and from the British Colonials that they were trying to separate from. The Second Amendment was then created to allow these settlers to defend themselves during those difficult times. However, it was vague, and that vagueness has since cost the lives of thousands of Americans, especially in the past ten years. We need change!"

As more applause rang out, a rapture of angry cries from certain politicians yelled out. The speaker tried to recapture control, but the room devolved into chaos. It took a long while until order was restored, but when it was, I realized that I may be stoking a fire I soon wouldn't be able to control.

"Well, it seems like we have an enormous amount to discuss about this topic." The speaker announced in a calm voice, looking around at Congress. "We will break the session for now and will reconvene when both sides have submitted plans for a compromise. What we will do before we leave though is vote on this problem. Use your keypads and vote on this. All in favour of re-examining the Second Amendment and restructuring it?"

My heart was racing as people made their votes. When the speaker called for those against, I was terrified as I saw a lot of the room move their hands. Would all my work be naught and fall at this all-important hurdle, after all I've been through?

After a few minutes, the speaker called out, "Alright, results have been counted. Yeas: 220. Nays: 215. The motion is passed, this proposal will go on through the system."

"Thank-you, your honours." I stated, backing down from the podium. My relief was so immense, I thought I would collapse right then and there. But as I was escorted out of the Capitol to my peeps, I knew I had to give one last announcement. When the front doors were opened, I was greeted by a wall of noise. The entire population of the Liberators camp was there, holding up signs and chanting words. As I came up to a smaller podium set up on the steps of the building, I cleared my throat and was waved in.

"My fellow protestors, I'm not sure if you were able to watch the TV while making our voices heard here, but here is the news from today's meeting." I said, hiding my growing elation. Then, to add drama, I paused. After a few seconds, I filled my lungs and shouted, "THEY PASSED IT! THEY'RE GOING TO AMEND THE AMENDMENT!"

A roar of happiness blasted me, and I was surprised the windows behind me didn't shatter. I had overcome another obstacle in preserving my dad's memory and getting some bit of revenge on Carl Fillmore. Now, with that hurdle overcome, it was time for the fourth and final round.

{ **19** }

A Leader's Work Is Never Done

<u>15th August 2021; 1136 hours</u>

It had been three weeks since our trip to Washington, and it had been a total success. When we returned to San Diego at the beginning of August, we tried to organize events nationwide as we watched C-SPAN, observing the government going through the process of amending the amendment.

I should have known, though, that the closeness of the vote was an indication. The debate on our issue was quickly becoming a drawn-out, lengthy ordeal, as both sides were producing more and more arguments to their sides of the decision. After the proceedings had reached the aforementioned three weeks, I'll admit, I was beginning to get worried.

My return to the surf shop, though, had given me a time to relax and straighten my thoughts. I also returned to surfing and swimming at Ocean Beach, and this really, *really* got me back to my normal life. Another thing that had allowed me to calm down was the fact that Travis had begun dating me. I decided that, while I would hold onto my memories of Colby and never forget him, I knew that Sam was right. Colby would want me to be happy, and Travis did just that in spades. The way that Travis and I began our close relationship made me laugh.

When I got home, the first thing I did with Sam was go surfing. As I crested the top of a massive swell and began to rip down the wave, my stress of the past melted right through my board. Suddenly, though, someone dropped in on me and knocked me right off my feet. As I plunged underwater, my anger flared up. Colby had taught me the rules and respects of surfing, and rule number one: once a wave is claimed, it is off-limits to everyone else. Dropping-in is very rude.

Surfacing, I slicked back my hair and yelled, "You *kook*! That wave was mine!"

The other surfer came up, and it turned out to be Travis. "I'm sorry, Nicole! Didn't see you there!"

"Oh!" I said quietly, climbing onto my board. I looked down at the Tonga board to hide my blushing. I had kept the board in good shape, and even stuck a waterproof copy of the picture Becky had of me and her on the head of the board. This way, I could preserve my memory of her and our fun times surfing at Ocean Beach. "That's...That's okay, Travis."

"Hey, you've been doing great work as of late." He said, paddling over to me. "I can't help but notice how you look on those podiums."

"Oh, and how *do* I look?" I asked, blushing.

"If I may be so brave," He reached over and kissed my salty cheek, "beautiful."

Looking at Travis in complete shock, I stammered, "You...you..."

"Yes, Nicole, I do." He said, and he hopped over onto my board, tilting us off. As we came back up, we were laughing hard. "And the work we've been doing lately has been drawing us closer. You are a remarkable young woman, Nicole, and I hope you don't find my previous action too bold."

As an answer, I reached over and we hugged each other, confirming our new relationship. My heart was aflutter, just as it had been when Colby and I first started dating. I was so happy, and I could feel Colby's spirit screaming out his approval.

***

A week later, which was a week of constant protests and handing out surfboards and tourist info, I decided to take one day off from campaigning and from work. Taking a picnic blanket and basket with us, Travis and I were sitting on the beach for the day. During this time, we surfed and watched people walk across the sand and go to and from the water. After a few hours of doing this, I sighed, I leaned my head against Travis' shoulder.

"Travis, am I dreaming?" I asked wistfully, closing my eyes. "This just seems too peaceful to be true."

"If you are dreaming, then you have a great imagination." He told me, his curly brown hair tickling my forehead. As

I opened my eyes, I looked straight into his amber-coloured eyes. He gently put an arm around my recovering shoulder and leaned his head against mine. "Keep it up. The world needs to be like this every day."

Giggling, I pecked Travis on the cheek and whispered in his ear, "I'll try."

As we turned our heads towards the water, we were quiet for a while, just savouring the moment. While people we knew passed by us and waved, we didn't say much to them. We just wanted to remain where we were and chill.

After we had a delicious lunch of ham sandwiches and fruit, someone came up from behind me and poked me in the back, causing me to start.

"Surprise!" Melissa shouted, laying down a blanket beside ours.

"Melly!" I cried, hugging my relative. "What are you doing here? I thought you were on a trip to Turkey for the next while!"

"Well, the place I was going to is under a serious fire warning this summer, so we were told to not come unless necessary. The university has decided to postpone the trip until next summer. So, my hubby and I just decided to come and visit my favourite cousin in her hometown! Mom's here too, but she's in Ocean Side visiting old friends and colleagues."

"Cool! Well, welcome to the Golden State!" I told her, mimicking the greeting she had given me in Vermont. "Oh, hey! This is my boyfriend, Travis. He's one of the members of the San Diego chapter for the Liberators. Travy, may I introduce Dr. Melissa Scott, my cousin from Vermont."

"Pleasure to meet you, sir." Melissa said, shaking his hand.

"Please, just call me Travis." My boyfriend chuckled, smiling. "I'm too chill to be called a 'sir' yet."

Laughing, Melissa replied, "I'll keep that in mind."

Looking around, I asked, "Where's Jay?"

"At the surf shop, getting us some boards."

"You know, I easily would have donated my board to you, cuz." I told her, indicating the Tonga board behind me.

Looking at the photo on the board, Melissa shook her head. "No, that is your board, and your board alone. It seems too important for you to just pass on to a newbie."

"Newbie?" I asked, giggling. "What a minute. Even with a family on the West Coast, you're a *kook*? You've *never* been surfing before?"

"Well, yes, I have been surfing." Melissa admitted, squirming a little in her bikini. "Just not enough to be good. You can't very much surf on Lake Champlain!"

Laughing hard, I said, "Agreed! Well, if you want some lessons, Travis here is an absolute master. He's won a few trophies in the surf competitions around SD."

"Aw, c'mon baby, don't scare your cousin." Travis reminded me, tickling my back a little. "You're making her feel like I'm too good for her."

Blushing, Melissa said, "Nah, I'm fine. If you want to teach me, and possibly Jay, then your trophy case is actually a good thing. Thanks!"

The rest of the afternoon was spent surfing and swimming in the ocean with my cousin and her husband. The day was perfect, with no clouds, perfect heat, and double overhead just kept coming and coming. It was pretty clear from the outset that Melissa had a little bit of experience in surfing, but Jay, who was an engineer from Wyoming, had no clue about the sport. He needed specific instruction from Travis, while Melissa and I crested a few waves. By the time the supper hour had arrived, we were all in a very happy mood.

As we made our way back up to the Miller house, we constantly smiled and joked, laughing up a kind of ruse that had become foreign in my life. With my starting university at UCSD in a few weeks, I realized that I needed to clear my mind and begin redeveloping my social life. I didn't necessarily know what I wanted to do, but I knew where I wanted to go.

"Knock, knock, we're back!" I called out when we got back to my house. "I've got a surprise."

"We do too, dear!" Mom called out from the kitchen. As the four of us split to change into dry clothes, Melissa and I went up to my room. When we got there, I saw an unfamiliar suitcase sitting on my bed.

"Wait, I thought you three were staying in a hotel?" I asked, my smile expanding.

"I never said which one!" Melissa pointed out, laughing. "Whenever we Vermonters arrive in the Golden State, we always refer to this place as a hotel. So, I did tell you the truth, just not the truth you expected!"

Hugging my cousin, I told her. "This is a perfect surprise to end a perfect day. Thank-you."

After we switched to some comfy t-shirts and shorts, we joined the boys, Izzy, and Mom in the dining room. Laughing at Mom's joke when she told me that we had ruined the surprise, we sat down and got straight to business consuming a delicious meal of steak and corn-on-the-cob. Mom then explained to us that, the next day, her company was submitting their final closing remarks on their case in the Supreme Court against the government. I had followed their progress and was confident that the government would have to waiver in the case, which would indeed be a massively historic outcome.

I tried not to focus on the topic though, as I didn't want it to ruin my mood. After dinner was swept away, our family and Travis began a massive game of team Trivial Pursuit, where Melissa and Jay absolutely killed us, taking the game in just ten rounds! As they clinked their segments together, my competitive anger came boiling up, and I challenged them to a rematch, this time a double game. Travis and I had come very close to winning, so I knew I had a very good shot. Melissa upped the stakes by saying that, if she won, I would have to surrender my bedroom for the rest of her stay.

"That's it?" I asked, grinning. "C'mon, cuz, dream big!"

"Alright, if you want me to up the stakes even further, so be it." She told me, cracking her knuckles. "If you lose, you give me the Tonga board."

Gasps rang across the room as everyone looked at me. Raising one of my eyebrows, I looked back at my cousin slyly. *Too rich for my blood?* I thought, as I mulled over the thought of losing the board. *Well, if she wants to play that high, she clearly doesn't know me too well.* "Okay, if you're going to raise the stakes that high, let's keep it even. If *I* win, you will pay for my college tuition for the first year! And I mean FULLY!"

A chorus of 'oooooohs' went around the table. Izzy looked shocked and she immediately signed, *You can't be serious, Nick! That's like $52, 000!*

"No, Mom, she may have a fair bet." Melissa rested her chin on her fists and looked deeply at me. After a few seconds of consideration, she said, "Very well. That board is equal in value, both monetarily and personally, so it is indeed a far bet. Shake on it?"

"You know it, Melly. You're on!" I declared, accepting my cousin's gesture.

Just then, a call came on my smartphone. As I went to answer it, I felt a sense of dread coming upon me. The only people who would have called me on my cell that late at night were the Liberators, and they rarely called with good news. As I answered the call, I heard that it was indeed Sam.

"Sammy, you're interrupting my family Trivial Pursuit game here. I've got a really big bet going here!"

"Sorry, Nick, but this is serious." Sam replied, her voice full of fear. "I've just gotten word that the government is releasing an argument that will help them beat us. You need to create a stir around the country so that their argument shows no merit and will stand like a two-legged chair."

I blanched at the news, my expression being noticed by my family and looks of concern reflect back at me. "You can't be serious. In one night? I may be a great orator, but I'm not *that* good!"

"Well, maybe it's time to show your true mettle in the

practice, my friend." Sam stated, her voice barely hiding signs of panic now. "If you don't, all of our work will be for naught."

"Fine, I'll deal with that tomorrow." I promised her. "Just let me finish off my cousin here, and then I'll get on with creating my speech for tomorrow. You contact everyone in the Liberators. Get anyone in California who can make it to Ocean Beach there tomorrow and gather everyone else in our sister cities. It's time for my ultimatum."

"Oh? Well, I can't wait to hear it." Sam said. "See you tomorrow."

"See you." I told her, hanging up. Returning to my chair, I explained the situation, and my family was sympathetic.

Is there anything I can do while I'm here? Izzy signed, her face strong.

"Call up everyone in Vermont." I ordered her firmly. "We'll need all the help we can get."

"You got it." Melissa responded, nodding.

"Izzy, I may need your help in writing a speech again, just like the one you had helped me with for my appearance in front of the House of Representatives." I explained. "This one will be just as crucial."

You can count on me. Izzy confirmed, looking happy that she can at least help in some way.

Taking a deep breath to calm myself down, I turned back towards Melissa. "Well, looks like all that's left for tonight is to beat you."

Are you sure that you should be doing that right now? Izzy asked, frowning. *I think you should focus your attention on this situation instead of playing a game.*

"I understand the importance of this, but I still need some time to rest, and besides, Melissa is about to lose, anyway!"

"Oh really? Well, you know, seeing as this is just about the two of us, let's make it *just* the two of us. No teams, no other players. Just you and me."

"You are *on*, Melly." I replied, grinning.

Okay, Nick, just keep in mind that you'll have a lot of work to do right after this. Izzy signed, eyeing me strongly.

As the game began, we discovered that we needed our teammates' help after all. The game took much longer than the first one, with both of us putting up great answers, just not the *right* ones every time. Soon, it came down to one question; if I got it right, I won, but if I got it wrong and Melissa got it right, I would lose.

"Alright, for the game and the wager, here is the question in the category of Movies and TV." Mom instructed me. "'Was Bonnie Tyler's song 'Holding out for a Hero' first released on the 'Footloose' movie soundtrack or on a separate album and then used on the subsequent soundtrack?'"

"On the soundtrack, *then* released on a separate album!" I shouted, ecstatic at my luck. "I win, cousin! You owe me my tuition."

"Hold it, I call foul!" Melissa shouted, holding up her hands. "That was *not* a fair question!"

"And why not, Ms. Sore Loser?" Travis teased, grinning.

"That's *Doctor* Sore Loser to you, dude, and I am protesting because Nicole was just in the musical Footloose! *And* she played the character that *sang* 'Holding out for a Hero! Of *course,* she would know that!"

"It was fair, and it was valid, Melly!" Mom reminded her. "Doesn't matter where you learned the answer, what matters is that you know it! You made the bet, you gotta pay up!"

"But...but..." Melissa stammered. Then she sighed. "Alright, very well. I concede defeat. Well done, my cousin."

"Yes!" I shouted, pumping my fist. "Redemption and a year's free education are mine! This day was great!"

{ 20 }

A Speech Like No Other

The next day started off not so great. I had not slept much the night before, so when I woke up there were shadows under my eyes, which proved to be an issue trying to conceal with makeup. Breakfast was a quiet affair, with everyone on edge with what was going to be done that day. After a long walk to Ocean Beach, Sam was working with Laura setting up a mic and plugging in the amplifiers and view screen.

I was standing backstage, feeling terrified. Laura's dad had built the stage for my rallies from a trashed pier, and it had been a great tool. While I waited for the rally to begin, I was being comforted by Mom and Izzy. Melissa and my siblings were out in the audience pumping the crowd up and making sure the media had their cameras trained on the stage. As I peeked above the surface and saw what I was dealing with, my heart leapt up into my throat.

"I don't know if I can do this." I admitted, feeling shaken. "The government's submission is very compelling to many people, and if I make just one mistake, my whole campaign will be over."

Hey, what's with all of these 'I's'? Quit feeling like you're alone! Izzy signed to me aggressively. *I can assure you one thing: The minute you* look *weakened, that's when you'll be eaten alive. Remember what the great Chinese philosopher Sun Tzu said:* When weak; act strong.

Swallowing back the fearful response I was about to give, I looked at Mom and she just nodded. Squaring my shoulders and taking a deep breath, I said, "Okay, I'm ready. Signal Sam that it's time for my speech."

Good luck. Izzy told me, patting me on the back as I climbed the steps of the stage. A massive roar met me as my friends and followers cheered me on. I got to the mic, addressed the reporters to start filming, and I began.

"Good morning, San Diego." I announced solemnly, trying to quiet the crowd. "I come before you in a state of urgency. I have received word that, as we speak, the U.S. Senate is releasing documents in a bill that show that they cannot conform to the demands we compromised with them. There is a series of Senators that do not wish to see the Second Amendment changed as we see fit, even though there was a majority ruling in our favour when we were in Washington just last month!"

As boos rang out and thumbs-down gestures appeared above the heads of many, I continued, building on the energy I was creating. "We have worked too hard and for too long on this campaign for it to falter on technicality! We need to tell the Senate now that that bill is a corrupt and outlandish ploy to slow us down, put out by those who are on the pay-roll of and in sponsorships with gun manufacturers and gun-support groups! That bill is being put out by people that are living in the past! If they pass it, it will degenerate and erode the very foundation of our government and give free-reign once again to those gun-wielders that go out and perform mass-shootings! We have lost too many innocent people in this nation for that to happen, and if it does, there will be even more deaths!"

Screams of protests rang out, and I realized that what I had just said was creating anger not just directed towards the government. I chose to ignore that and soldier on. "What will it take for these policy-makers to realize that every life lost in America due to uncontrolled gun violence is a life too many? Will it take the death of one of their own to realize that? But wait, that's damn-near happened already! Gabrielle Giffords nearly died because of this violence, and when she began advocating, people listened. But her voice was lost in the government she once was a part of when the bureaucrats stepped in and muzzled her.

"Now, she has a new partner, and she is standing right in front of you. I stand before you and am telling you that I refuse to be muzzled! I intend to make sure that even if there is another opportunity to kill a government official via gunshots, it will never succeed. But the only way that that assurance can be secured is if the government refuses to pass their document. So, I'm in front of you now, asking you all one question. Who here wishes to see that bill passed?"

Crickets sounded as a blanket of silence suddenly

enveloped the crowd. I looked around, and only heard the sound of the waves breaking. I half-expected the lobbyists to come out again and try to stop me, but nobody came. After a few seconds to let the response sink in, I finished. "Just as I thought. I look now at the government and ask this again: how many have to die before a change in this law comes around? HOW MANY? HOW MANY?" The chant continued as the crowd picked it up. As I was satisfied that my point was made and there was nothing left for me to say, I gestured for the reporters to begin their pieces to the news.

Stepping back from the mic, I suddenly got a call from one of those reporters. She gestured for me to come over to her, and when I did, I saw that she was showing me a broadcast of the president in the Senate chamber. I told her to wait, then got the seventy-inch TV screen Laura's dad installed above the podium changed to the right channel. The chanting stopped as I hooked up the audio.

"...you just saw, my fellow representatives, Nicole Miller is not a girl that can be brought down by something as frivolous and fraudulent as that document." The president was saying. "And she is absolutely correct. Gabrielle Giffords was one of your most esteemed colleagues in the House of Representatives, and she was nearly assassinated by a sniper! By releasing that bill and passing it, you will be soiling her legacy and her courageous efforts, as well as soiling the memories of every victim of mass shootings since Columbine!

"Nicole Miller nearly gave her own life trying to save her classmates and their families in the Lincoln High Shooting but was unsuccessful. To redeem herself emotionally, she took up a mantle of leadership to prevent a similar tragedy from happening again, and when her efforts began, there hadn't been a major firearms death anywhere in these fifty states! Then, when her work took a break, Vermont suffered a terrible loss at Christmas, right in front of Ms. Miller herself!

"She then returned with a vigor to her campaign, and the country once again went quiet. The minute you put that bill into practice, we will be right back in the middle of a crisis, and possibly a worse one then in the one we were in before! This country has begun to feel safe thanks to Nicole Miller, but if that document goes through, that feeling will snap like a willow branch and we'll spiral into absolute chaos! If that chaos happens, I will resign from office and you will be forced to fend for yourselves!"

As cheers went up from my crowd at the president's harsh words towards the Senate, she continued. "Actually, before I surrender my post, I'd make sure that the bill is forcibly removed from enactment, so that I can leave with a clear conscience, which I feel a lot of you do not have. If this is what the democracy of the U.S. has boiled down to, then our country is no longer functioning as such. It is now just one big company more interested in money than in the interests of Americans.

"From what I have seen and am seeing, it apparently doesn't matter to the government how many of our fellow Americans die due to gun violence, just as long as an outdated concept continues, and citizens get to maintain a ridiculous image of importance and 'coolness' with their firearms. In terms of the people in government themselves, as long as they receive their allotted money from gun manufacturers and gun-support groups, they're happy. If that's what the government I'm in charge of wants, then I will indeed resign and have nothing to do with it anymore. Thank-you, America, and thank-you Nicole Miller. You have served your country as much as your father did, and he would be proud of you. You have officially stepped out of his shadow and become a strong, confident, independent young woman. Wherever you are, I hope you are listening, and know that you have my support for your cause."

As the president stood back, more applause and cheers echoed across the beach. As we continued to watch the screen, the screen split and we saw protests rising in Kansas City, New Orleans, Seattle, Burlington, Indianapolis, as well as a drone-shot of our massive protest. My heart soared as I learned that my efforts are showing the country that we will not be ignored. *What have I done?* I thought as I realized that my one voice had expanded to millions across the country.

After a few minutes of the TV anchors talking about the speech and updating their audience, focus returned towards the Senate and the buzz going around it. As order was called, the Senate came together and decided to skip the formalities (for once) and get straight on to voting on passing the bill. My heart was racing in anticipation, and I knelt beside Sam to try and calm down. Izzy and Mom came up and stood beside us, with Mom putting a hand on my shoulder in sympathy. When I stood back up, we all joined hands as the vote was finished.

"The motion is confirmed. Yay votes: zero. Nay votes: fifty. The vote is unanimous. This bill will not pass, and the original changes to the Second Amendment have now officially been passed by the U.S. Senate. There will be a twenty-eighth amendment to the constitution."

Windows rattled on the surf shop as a thunderous roar came from the crowd. As the TV image showed the other cities, bucketful after bucketful of confetti was streaming through downtown Burlington, there were thousands of cheering people in New Orleans, making Mardi Gras look like a low-key birthday party, and a gigantic American Flag was being carried over the top of the massive crowd in Seattle. I was so relieved, I nearly collapsed to the sand. I had accomplished everything I wanted and then some.

"We did it!" Sam screamed beside me, jumping up and down. "We did it, we did it, we did it!"

As I stared into my aunt and adopted mother's eyes, I couldn't help but feel a sense of satisfaction. "I guess we did it." I breathed, feeling incredibly relaxed.

"No, Nick." Mom said, shaking her head and hugging me. "*You* did it."

{ **21** }

Reflection: An Autobiography

<u>23rd April 2040; 0800 hours</u>

"Alright, kids, time for school!" I called out, gathering up my children's lunch kits.

As Robert, Gabrielle, and Rebecca shot up from their seats at the kitchen table, Travis came over and kissed me on the cheek. He then ran his hand through my hair, which had a few strands of gray developing in it. My glasses were jostled as he removed his hand, and we hugged closely for a second. Travis then smiled at me, and I returned the gesture.

"Gotta run, babe. I've got six beachcombers to teach before ten." He told me quietly, reaching around me and picking up his own lunch and his travel mug.

"Be home for supper. It's pizza night, you know!" I reminded my husband, smoothing his 'official work uniform', which consisted of a full-sized swimsuit and flip-flops; that day, Travis was teaching surfing, swimming, and scuba-diving at his family's surf shop, which he and Laura had inherited from their dad three years before.

"Hey, like I'd miss Justice Nicole Bews' famous homemade four-cheese pizza!" He responded, kissing me again. He then took off. "See ya, my sweet!"

"Bye!" I told him, turning back to my kids. "Okay, guys, go brush your teeth, grab your backpacks, and I'll meet you at the van. We leave in ten minutes!"

"You got it mommy!" Rebecca squeaked, and the three of them took off. As I looked out at them, I couldn't help but smile. Robert was eight, Gabrielle was seven, and little Rebecca was just five. They were all in school at Longfellow Elementary, and though it was exhausting at times, it was still pretty awesome to have kids.

Trying hard to not think of the laundry list of cases I would have to go through that day, I decided to look into the past, something I regularly did as I raised my family. I decided to start at what happened right after the historic vote.

***

<u>19th August 2021; 1300 hours</u>

"I can't believe we did it." I say, shaking my head.

I am standing in the University Centre of UCSD, and I'm watching a newsfeed on one of the main lobby's TV screens. It's showing the president signing the Twenty-Eighth Amendment into law, and my internal jaw is on the floor as I reflected on where I came from and what I had done. As they pull me along, I continue to walk with Mom and Jamie. They're escorting me to an interview with the Dean of the Faculty of Law and are happy to be with me at such a major event. I had decided on my future after our victory beach party a few days before, and I felt that it would be fitting to follow in Mom's footsteps and become a lawyer. I just felt a little saddened that Dad couldn't be here to witness this, but I knew he was with me in spirit.

"Well, believe it, Nick." Jamie tells me as we walk down a crowded hallway. I feel multiple sets of eyes gazing upon me as I pass, most of them I notice are watching in awe. "It happened."

"And tomorrow is when the judges deliver their verdict on the lawsuit, so we'll find out if that victory is complete. My partners are on pins and needles in anticipation." Mom points out, a confident smile on her face. "But for now, let's focus on getting you into law school. I have a feeling you'll be a shoo-in in light of recent events."

"Cheers, Mom." I say, grinning.

Twenty minutes later, a smile is a long way from my mind as I'm sitting in front of the dean, his eyes almost looking right through me. He's a tall, thin, balding man in his late sixties, with blue eyes behind horn-rimmed glasses. His brown suit and expressionless face, to me, shows that he's all-business today. I'm sitting and sweating as I awaited his first question, sure that the fancy white blouse and knee-length blue skirt I'm dressed in are getting really, really smelly. On top of that, I'm wearing sparkling blue high-heels, and I don't know what is making me more uncomfortable, the heels, or the dean.

"So, Ms. Miller, I have reviewed your record, and I am very impressed. Your GPA was 3.9, with your highest classes in your senior grade. Did you feel that you had to struggle, or did you feel you were able to cruise through them?"

All It Takes Is One

"Actually sir, I felt it was somewhere in the middle. I didn't exactly have to struggle, but I definitely didn't cruise through them. I took my time with my assignments and made sure I put a lot of effort into my work. I expect that I will have to put a lot more into my work if I am permitted into your school."

After another pause, the dean looks at me with a new expression, this one with his bushy gray eyebrows higher and the faintest trace of a smile in his lips. "Interesting response, Ms. Miller. What would your focus of study be if you were permitted into our faculty?"

"I would probably focus on firearms cases and on cases related to the Twenty-Eighth Amendment."

"Well, I'm glad you brought that up." The dean says, a smile now fully on his face, followed by a twinkle in his eye. "This is the real reason I decided to meet up with you myself. Do you believe that what you learned in your campaign makes up for the fact that you did not take law-studies in twelfth grade?"

This time taking a few minutes to ponder my answer, I don't answer immediately. My palms are wet, and I can feel sweat falling down my forehead. Then, after a few seconds, I say, "For the most part, yes. I have seen how the government system works, how the judiciary system operates, and how laws are created and amended. I believe that, for the most part, it makes up for my lack of credit. What I didn't learn I feel I can do so in my free time during the semester."

A look of satisfaction on his face, the dean nods. "Then in light of recent events and in what I have heard here, I can say, despite your late application and your lack of certain credits, you will be fully accepted into the University of California San Diego's School of Law. Welcome to college, Ms. Miller!"

"*Thank-you very much, sir!*" *I say, shaking the dean's hand. "I'll see you in a few weeks for Welcome Week!*"

I then stand up and walk out. As I got out into the waiting room, I started leaping up and down. "I did it! I did it! They let me in!"

"Well done, Nick!" Mom cries, hugging me hard. "I knew you could do it!"

"All that's left is for Mom to win her case, and my life will be perfect!" I say, finishing it off with an almighty whoop.

***

<u>20th August 2021; 0945 hours</u>

The next day, I'm sitting in our living room with Jamie, Allan, Travis, Moon, and Jack as we all watch the results of the Supreme Court's decision. When the judges walked in, I felt my heart leap, and I grip Travis' hand hard and tight.

"The court is now in session." The head judge's voice rings out. "The case presented today is Miller v. The Department of Homeland Security. Both parties have presented their sides, and the court has come to deliver its verdict."

After a small pause, the judge continues. "It is the decision of this court, after much deliberation, that the Department of Homeland Security was indeed unsuccessful in ensuring the safety of Americans within the borders of our nation. Thus, Theresa Miller's suit of seven hundred and eighty-five million dollars allocated to shooting victims will be allowed. The distribution of the funds shall be decided at a later date."

"Yes!" I shout, pumping my fists as Jack takes off from my lap. "We won!"

All It Takes Is One

"We did indeed." Allan says, gripping the picture of Becky that normally sits in his room. "Retribution is ours at last. History has been made, again."

***

So, with those events in my life, I felt things couldn't be better, but they did. As a reward for my bravery in the shootings and all my hard work in my campaign, the president bestowed upon me something I felt I never would have earned: The Presidential Medal of Honour. I was reluctant to accept it at first, but Aunt Izzy pressed me to do it, and when I did, the press declared me a national hero.

Gun laws became stricter, and though there were a slew of people fighting to reverse the changes, the government reminded them that the old rules had led to too many deaths in the United States, and that they were treating it as a national crisis. This meant that no matter what protests came to renounce the new agreement, it could not be overturned. I constantly smiled as I saw the bands of protestors get smaller and smaller as this sank in over the span of many weeks.

After that, though things were long over, the media kept swarming me, trying to see what I would take on as my next cause. But all the fame involved with my campaign had been overwhelming, so I decided to hide from the public eye for a while and get down to my studies.

I graduated five years after the Washington rally with a first-class honours degree in law from UCSD and began practicing at Mom's office. Six years after that, I applied to be a judge in San Diego County Court, and I was immediately accepted, working on trials that specifically had to do with guns and the laws I fought hard to create and change. At the same time, Travis had graduated with a degree in oceanography, and worked with a research group watching the local bays. He only worked this job seasonally, so he still ran the Ocean Beach surf shop with Laura to keep him busy during the off-season.

In Sam's case, instead of becoming an actual nurse, she went on to become a television actress, starring in various hospital dramas that we all watched with great enthusiasm. She always came back to SD, though, as she never wanted to live in LA and its hectic lifestyles. She and Jeff got engaged a year after we graduated, and they enjoyed a wonderful life together.

***

21ˢᵗ *August 2031; 2236 hours*

In 2031, we travel to Las Vegas to celebrate the tenth-year anniversary of our victory. During that time, another surprise comes to me. We are staying in Caesar's Palace and are having the time of our lives. One night, we decide to head over to Vegas' iconic sky-wheel, the High Roller, to get some great shots of the Strip and the surrounding hotels. When our capsule is at its peak, I take a shot of our hotel, and when I turn back to Travis, he's down on one knee and has a spectacular diamond and sapphire ring pointing right up at me.

"I know it's taken a long time, but I think we can make this work now. Nicole Miller, will you marry me?"

I am so taken aback by the gesture, I faint right then and there.

When I come to, at the bottom of the ride, I feel like I had just jumped from the top of ride instead of riding it.

The first words out of my mouth are ones that change my life as much as the campaign.

"I do, dude." I say weakly, smiling up at a completely surprised Travis. He then looks relieved and helps me to my feet. He then slides the ring on my finger, and we kiss passionately.

As we get off the capsule and I show off my ring to the rest of my friends at the anniversary party, everyone is ecstatic. Sam, who is in the middle of a shoot for a Rom-Com, says that she has had inspiration for her role. My mom, who is accompanying us and is nearing her retirement, says she feels so proud and so happy for me. It is another time I know that, though he is gone, my dad is looking down on me with his trademark wide smile.

***

23<u>rd</u> October 2032; 1121 hours

On a barge in the middle of Lake Champlain, I am being escorted down the aisle by Jamie. The scenery around our wedding ceremony is just gorgeous, as we had decided to hold it during the changing of the colours. I am staring straight ahead at Travis, who looks uncomfortably impeccable in his tuxedo. Allan is right beside him, along with the rest of my brothers. Sam is waiting for me on the other side, wearing a very sweet looking dress. My dress is narrow but beautiful, mainly made up of white silk and lace.

When I get up to the front, Jamie kisses my forehead and says, "Good luck, Nick. And thank you."

As he sits down and the ceremony begins, we enjoy calm waters *and bright blue skies. When we get to our vows, I look deep into Travis' eyes and say the most important speech I have ever given.*

"Travis Bews. You have been my love since my senior year, and ever since I have been unable to think of a person I want to be with more. You are my rock, my core, my friend. I vow to be with you for the rest of time, and never have anyone else."

As Sam tilts her head in appreciation, I feel strong. After a few seconds, Travis begins his vows. "Nicole Miller. The minute I saw you, the first night you surfed at Ocean Beach twelve years ago, I knew there was something between us. When we hit it off, literally hit it off, I knew right then and there that I had found the woman I was meant to be with. As you worked yourself through college, you showed that you were a brilliant, beautiful woman. Then, when we went to Vegas, I felt right then that it was time. It was then I decided you were the woman I will forever love, and no one else will take me away from you."

As the audience applauds, the priest asks us a set of questions that every woman imagines she'll answer.

"Do you, Travis Bews, welcome Nicole Miller as your wife, offering her your love and encouragement, your trust and respect, as together you create your future?"

Travis squares his shoulders, and, looking into my eyes, says, "I do."

"Do you, Nicole Miller, welcome Travis Bews as your husband, offering him your love and encouragement, your trust and respect, as together you create your future?"

My heart pounding, I say, "I do."

"Then, by the power invested in me, I now pronounce you husband and wife. You may kiss."

All It Takes Is One

As Travis and I embrace each other, maple leaves coloured brilliant red fall upon us, and a series of white doves are released. We then have a great reception at the Miller family farm, complete with my brothers doing country renditions of some of our favourite songs. My life is perfect.

***

A little while after that, a little gift called Robert Colby Bews arrived, and he turned my life even more into paradise. Don't get me wrong. Being a mother is never, EVER easy, but I was still enjoying it, plus I had a big family behind me, always willing to help. The following year, we had Gabrielle, whom I had named after my favourite hero during the campaign. Her middle name was Isabella, after my favourite aunt. By the time Rebecca Theresa arrived, things had gotten crowded in our small suburban house in Chula Vista, so we moved back into La Jolla, close to the 'Miller Hotel'.

Keeping in contact with our family and the massive friendship circle we had accrued through the campaign, Travis and I lived a lively, yet quiet life in California, with frequent trips to Vermont to visit family. We also still went to Ocean Beach, helping out Laura whenever and wherever we could.

There was one thing that I did do during my marriage that garnered me new fame, but not for long. It was indeed a new cause, but not a political one. It was a cause from the heart. Together with Colby's parents, Don and Robyn Anderson, we formed the Colby Anderson Memorial Reef Fund in honour of Colby's lifelong ambition. I remembered from our first night together on Ocean Beach where Colby told me he wanted to be a biologist and save the reefs *off the coasts of Australia and New Zealand. Because of this, I felt it was the best way for me to fully honour my lost love for Colby by forming a non-profit organization that partnered with groups like Green Peace to help save the coral reefs in the Andersons' home country. With that, my conscious was finally cleared.*

***

"C'mon, mommy, let's go!" Rebecca said excitedly, pulling my arm towards the door and me out of my memories.

"I'm coming, baby, I'm coming!" I told her, grabbing my keys and my own lunch kit. "Now, everybody got everything?"

"Yes, mom." Came a chorus of responses. As I entered and opened the garage, we loaded into my minivan and started off. When we were stopped at a red light a few minutes later, Robert asked me a question.

"Mommy, I have to write a speech to read to my class next week. Can you help me with it?"

Smiling, I had to bite my lip to prevent a giggle from escaping. I hadn't yet shared my experiences with my kids, or the real reason why there were awards and medals all over my office. I just wanted to be Mommy to them, not a legendary character that they stood in awe of. "Of course, sweetie." I replied, looking in the rear-view mirror at my son. "I'd love to help. In fact, speeches are something I used to be pretty good at."

The End

The End

Family Trees

Miller Family Tree
By: Rebecca Miller

Angus William Miller (1939 – 2011) – Elizabeth Blanche McKay (b. 1940)

Children of Angus and Elizabeth:
James Angus (b. 1960) (m. Isabella Jones [b. 1961])
Jameson "Jamie" William (b. 1962) (m. to Theresa Armstrong [b. 1962])
Jennifer "Jenna" Blanche (b. 1964) (m. to Adam Simon [b. 1960])

Children of James and Isabella:
Patrick Roger (b. 1988) (e. to Andrea McConnell [b. 1990])
Dr. Melissa Alexandra (b. 1994) (m. to Jay Scott [b. 1994])
Alison Dawn (b. 1995) (e. to Mark Docherty [b. 1996])
Colin Frank (b. 2002 [twin to Colleen])
Colleen Francine (b. 2002 [twin to Colin])

Children of Jameson and Theresa:
Marcus Lawrence (b. 1990 [twin to Samuel]) (m. to Tana Phillips [b. 1991])
Samuel Joseph (b. 1990 [twin to Marcus]) (m. to Janet Parenteau [b. 1992])
Anthony Maxwell (b. 1997)
Allan Ryan (b. 2001)
Rebecca Jane (2003 - 2020)
Nicole Adrianna (b. 2003) *

Children of Jennifer "Jenna" and Adam:
Jacob Charles (b. 1992 [twin to Jeremy) (m. to Sarah Villeneuve [b. 1994])
Jeremy Abraham (b. 1992 [twin to Jacob]) (m. to Hailey Burton [b. 1993])

Children of Marcus and Tana
Brennan Richard (b. 2016)
Brianne Lily (b. 2017)

Children of Samuel and Janet
Susan Anita (b. 2015)
Dennis Ryan (b. 2017)

Children of Patrick and Andrea
Andrew Glenn (b. 2017)

Children of Jacob and Sarah
Brayden George (b. 2017)

Children of Jeremy and Hailey
Thalia Tamara (b. 2018)

*Adopted

Armstrong Family Tree
By Rebecca Miller

Albert Thomas Armstrong (1941 – 2009) – Marion Catherine
Bradley (1943 – 2010)

Children of Albert and Marion:
Theresa Marion (b. 1962) (m. to Jameson Miller [b. 1962])
Kelly Valerie (b. 1969) (m. to Parker MacGregor [b. 1967])

Children of Theresa and Jameson: (See Miller Family Tree)

Children of Kelly and Parker:
Daniel Eric (b. 1998)

Colby's New Zealand Slang

Mate: Friend or enemy (depending on the speaker's tone)
Bra: Female equivalent of bro
Choice As: That's great, awesome, sure
You right?: Are you ok? Is everything ok?
Wanna Hiding?: Do you want to fight?
My Crib: My home or house
Bowl Round: Come over to visit
Slog: Work or shift
Chur: Thanks
Loo: bathroom
Gidday: Hello
Togs: Swimsuit or bathing suit
Straight up?: Are you telling the truth?

Acknowledgements

I would love to recognize my family and friends in helping me write this story. They helped develop the characters and the plot, as well as give me valuable support when it was needed the most. I got the inspiration for this story from seeing all the news stories about the gun violence in the United States and Canada and thinking about what would happen if just one person came out and rallied everyone around her to end gun violence. Things went from there, with me creating the most enjoyable and loving story I could. I hope you enjoyed this story, and if you are feeling like you want to speak out about something, remember, you always have a voice.

Born and raised around literature, Hayden W. DeGrow first wanted to write a book of his own when he was just six years old. Known by his family and friends as a great storyteller, DeGrow always loved imagining different worlds that he could tell other people about. Originally from Regina, Saskatchewan, he resides in Yorkton, Saskatchewan, where he works as a teacher and tutor, using his storytelling skills to engage his students.